McCabe's Land

ALSO BY PATRICK LINDSAY

McCabe's Land

Jake McCabe
Book Three

Patrick Lindsay

WOLFPACK
PUBLISHING
— EST 2013 —

McCabe's Land

Chapter 1

Vigilantes

KERRVILLE, TEXAS, 1874

They were ramming the doors outside the county jail. It sounded like they'd gone out and found themselves a log, and now they were pounding away with it. The doors rattled and shook with each blow. I wasn't sure those doors would hold up much longer. I glanced over at Boone, my deputy. He was, like me, crouched behind the sheriff's desk with a Winchester resting over the top. Neither one of us knew if we were willing to use those guns when the crowd broke through.

There was another blow at the doors, and Boone shifted his weight, getting down on his knees and sighting along the barrel. "I never knew a man," he said conversationally, "that could get hisself into so much trouble. You just got a knack for it, I reckon."

I'd known for years that arguing with Boone was a total waste of time. The thing was, I wasn't inclined to argue with him on this one. Danged if I know how I do it, but I do seem to wind up in a jam too much of the time. McCabe's luck, they used to call it. My wife Julia claims that all changed to good luck when I came to Texas and married her.

Now don't get me wrong, those things were good luck, sure enough. More luck than I deserved, according to Boone, but who's listenin' to him, anyway? The thing is, Julia would tell you I'm an uncommon, stubborn man, and sometimes that causes me some problems.

Take right now, for instance. This isn't even the county where I'm the sheriff. My county is Gillespie County and I make my home in Fredericksburg, about twenty-five miles down the trail from here. Kerrville is in Bexar County, where they've got themselves a different sheriff.

That could make a man wonder what I'm doing here, hunkered down behind a desk and tryin' to decide whether or not I'm gonna take a shot at that lynch mob out there, once they break down these doors.

Boone was wondering these same things, it was pretty clear. "Tell me again, McCabe, why we're fixin' to get our tails shot off for that crooked sheriff back there." He jerked a thumb in the direction of the cells, down the hall and around the corner.

There was another loud thud as they rammed the doors again with the log, or whatever that was they were using out there to batter things with. I cast a nervous eye at the doors, then relaxed just a smidge when they didn't fly open. Not this time, anyway.

"First off," I said, "it ain't up to us to decide whether that's an actual crooked sheriff back there. Way they explained it to me, our job is to bring him in and let the judge and the jury and such decide."

Boone snorted so loud I jumped just a little, then settled back down behind the desk. "I've done decided," he told me. "I've heard plenty. I'm thinkin' that if we let those folks out there get at him, it'll just save the judge some time."

Just then, a rock came flying through the window in the front of the jail. The glass shattered and flew across the front half of the sheriff's office. The rock rolled across the floor and stopped when it thumped against the back wall.

I half-rose and blew out the lantern in front of me, leaving the office in darkness. Just enough light to see the front doors. I knew they would have torches and lanterns out there. Plenty of light to see them when they burst in.

"Cover the window," I told Boone. "I'll cover the doors."

Boone shifted just slightly to train the rifle barrel on the broken window. "It don't make no difference, ya know," he rasped. "They'll get him an' string him up, whether or not they stretch our hides first."

"Actually," I told Boone, "they might not get him after they break in here. Depends on what we do."

I could almost feel Boone's stare boring into the side of my head. "There's about ten of them and two of us," he reminded me. "How d'ya figger?"

"Sheriff Richards ain't back there," I said. "He's not in the cell."

Finally, Boone pulled himself together enough to ask the question. "I know there ain't a lot of light back there," he said, "but what's that lump under the blanket I saw?"

"Just a lump," I told him. "I wadded up a blanket and put it under the top blanket. I put a rag doll on top of the pillow. It might fool 'em long enough for us to get out of here. I hid Sheriff Richards at the livery stable, down under a pile of hay, tied him down good. He's not going anywhere until we come for him."

There was a tearing sound coming from the front doors the next time they rammed it with the log.

"Okay, Cap'n," said Boone slowly. "I shoulda known you'd be a couple jumps ahead of me. You just hum the tune, an' I'll join in on the chorus."

———

THREE DAYS EARLIER

Finally, it seemed like the sheriff's job was settling down to what I'd expected when I took it a little over a year ago. The ranchers down south of here had settled a dispute about water, and the hired gunhands were gone. The cells in my jail were empty most days, like today, and I only had to toss a whiskeyed-up cowboy in the jail on a few Saturday nights when they got a little carried away.

The door to the jail/office opened and closed quietly, and I looked up to see my bride, Julia, carrying in my lunch. I cleared off the desk, she spread out the food, gave me a kiss, and I tied into the vittles. After about twenty minutes, I sat back with a sigh and thought about how good life was these days.

The fact that my deputy, Boone, had the day off today made things pretty quiet, and I leaned back in the chair, trying not to doze. I saw Julia watching me, and I knew that look. I brought my feet down off the desk and looked at her.

"You have some bad news, don't you?" I asked.

She shrugged and looked away, then looked back

around at me. "I'm not sure if what I heard is true," she started, dragging the words out slowly. "If what I heard is true, then it's bad news."

I nodded impatiently, waiting for her to get on with it.

"It's about the holdups over around Kerrville," she said, "and about the new sheriff over there in Bexar County."

I leaned my elbows on the desk and watched her face, thinking about what I knew about the sheriff in the county next door to mine. The old sheriff, Rolf Bergen, had been easing toward retirement for a few years already when I took over as sheriff in my county. He kinda came at trouble sideways, not wanting to stir things up right before he stepped down. He had finally retired just a few months ago.

The new sheriff was named Abe Richards, and his election seemed like a bit of a surprise to people over in Kerrville. I had never talked to the man, but I'd heard he was young and maybe likely to shoot first and ask questions later. I had enough territory to cover here in my county, so I minded my own business. Up until now, anyway. I stared at Julia uneasily, waiting.

"You know about the stagecoach holdups and the robbery at the general store in Kerrville, right?" she asked.

I leaned forward a little more, not liking the churning I was feeling in my gut. "I knew about the stagecoach robberies," I agreed. "Heard nothin' about a general store holdup."

"It happened yesterday," she said. "There were people talking about it at the bank when I stopped there this morning."

I nodded, still waiting for the news she'd avoided giving me so far.

"What I heard at the bank," she said, "is that some folks trailed the robbers out of town and kept watch when they holed up, several miles down the trail, acting like they were waiting for somebody."

"Wait," I interrupted, "what about the new sheriff, Richards, was he there with them?"

"No," she answered. "That's where the news gets worse. They didn't trust Richards, so he wasn't with them. They waited, watching to see if the robbers were going to meet up with anybody. When somebody finally rode up and joined them, it was the sheriff. Abe Richards."

"He's a part of the robberies?" I stammered, not able to believe it.

"That's what they think." Julia nodded. "Now there's talk, from what I heard, about forming up a posse and stringing up Richards."

I stared at the desk, trying to piece this together in my head. Stringing up a sheriff sounded like a real bad idea to me, seeing as how I am one. Still, if Richards was running a ring of bandits, it wasn't unheard of. And hanging the crooked sheriff is generally how these things turned out.

I looked up to see Julia's eyes on me, watching me like a hawk. "I told you because you needed to hear it, but I'm afraid of what you're going to do," she admitted. "If you decide to get in the middle of this, I know you. You won't let go until it's settled to your satisfaction. I don't want you getting strung up along with Richards."

Well, now, she had a point there. A real good point, I had to admit. The truth is, I didn't know what to do. I thought about my Texas Ranger pal, Captain Leander McNelly. I would have liked to have a sit-down with him about this, but they had sent him up north to deal with a Comanche uprising near the Palo Duro Canyon.

Julia's eyes were still on me, and I didn't feel good about any of my possibilities. I shrugged and slumped back in my chair. "I don't know what to do," I admitted. "I don't want to see that sheriff strung up, for sure I don't want to see it without an arrest and trial. But," I admitted reluctantly, "it's not really my fight."

I spread my fingers on the desk and stared at them. "I've got to think on it," I said finally. "I won't do anything without talking to you again first," I promised.

Julia nodded, stood, and gathered up what was left of my lunch. "Okay, that's good," she agreed. She gave me a kiss and moved over to the door, where she paused. "If you go over there," she said, "don't go without Boone."

"I agree with that, too," I said.

She nodded and opened the door. "I'll see you at supper," she told me.

I listened to her footsteps moving away, and I knew she'd given me another great piece of advice. Boone could be a chatterbox and a pain sometimes, but he was a great man to have in your corner when trouble comes. I wouldn't step foot in Bexar County without Boone.

———

Boone arrived the next morning like he usually does, throwing the front door to the office open so hard it bounced off the wall. I jumped, like I do sometimes when I don't see him comin', but this time, I was pouring myself the first cup of coffee for the day. I jumped so hard I spilled some hot coffee in my hand.

I set the cup down, hopped around a little, and commenced to talking in ways Julia don't approve of. After a while, I settled down some and glared at Boone, which I knew was a waste of time.

Boone settled down in the chair next to my desk and promptly put his boots up on the desk. I had to allow for the fact Boone was more'n old enough to be my daddy, so I just sat myself down and slurped at the coffee.

"What's goin' on, boss?" he asked breezily.

"What's goin' on," I said, "is that a mob might be fixing to take over in Kerrville, and they might hang themselves a sheriff over there."

The smile disappeared from Boone's face, and his boots thumped down on the floor as he sat forward. "Tell me about it," he said grimly.

I told him everything Julia had told me yesterday. There hadn't been any more news when I had gone home last night. Boone soaked up every word I said, looking more and more grim all the time.

"We cain't have a mob just down the road, hanging themselves a sheriff and mebbe a deputy too," he drawled. "Especially not after you an' me both just hauled off and got ourselves hitched."

I still couldn't quite believe that anybody had married Boone, but a gracious lady named Alice Brenham had done just that not long ago, just a few weeks after Julia and I were married.

"Good point," I agreed. "Sometimes you can get a mob with a thirst for blood. I don't know," I admitted, "just when I should or shouldn't get involved."

Boone pulled at his chin and stood up to prowl around the office. "What about yore Ranger buddy, McNelly?" he asked, screeching to a stop and turning around to look at me.

I shook my head. "No good," I told him. "He's up north at the Palo Duro Canyon. I could," I admitted, "send a telegram over to Austin. But," I concluded, "I don't know anybody else over there, and it might be too late by the time they get around to sending somebody."

Boone slumped back down in the chair and nodded. "Hmmph," was all he said. I could tell we were both out of ideas.

I heard a thumping sound on the boardwalk outside, and I knew it was the sound of my father-in-law, Ike Hawkins, coming to pay me a visit. He had lost a leg during the war and I could always hear that wooden leg thumping down.

The door was flung open, only a little less loud than Boone had done it earlier, and Ike stumped in, followed by Julia.

"There's a mob grabbed the sheriff, over to Kerrville," Ike thundered. "I know a guy with a ranch outside Kerrville. I've sold him a few cows ever' now and then. He sent a rider this morning to tell me they've got Abe Richards, holding him in the jail. They've got a couple boys sittin' on him over there, while the rest of 'em decide what to do with him."

Ike slumped into a chair and leveled his gaze at me. "Come sundown," he said, "they'll be likkered up enough they'll be likely to decide to stretch his neck."

I swung my gaze from Ike to Julia to Boone. I stood and walked over to my gun rack to take out my Winchester '73, then checked to be sure I had belted my

Colt on. Boone picked up his rifle and trailed after me to the door.

I stopped to kiss Julia in the doorway. "I can't stand by and see a man hung without arrest and trial," I told her. "Especially not another sheriff."

"I know," she murmured. "Just be careful and come home when you can."

———

That had been just this morning, when I'd said goodbye to Julia. It seemed like several days. I looked over at Boone. He had one eye on me and the other on the front door, which I knew was gonna come bustin' open at any minute.

"What are we gonna do?" Boone asked, one hand resting on his Colt and the other holding onto his Winchester.

"We let 'em come streaming in here," I said. I hung up the keys to the cells on a hook where anybody could see them. "Keep your hands away from your guns," I advised. "They're going to be in a big hurry to roust Richards out of that cell. The minute they go past us, we're out the front door."

Boone scratched his chin while a smile slowly spread across his face. "You want me to get the horses," he drawled.

I nodded. We had left the horses in an alley behind the livery stable, which was about two blocks down the street. Both horses were saddled and ready to go, along with a pack horse I'd brought with us.

"Bring our horses around to the side of the livery stable," I told him. "I'll haul Richards out of there, and we're gonna hit the trail for Fredericksburg in a mighty big hurry."

Boone was still grinning. "And the pack horse?" he asked.

"Richards is coming with us," I said. "He's just not gonna come in style, that's all."

The front doors flew open and slammed back against the walls of the sheriff's office. I counted seven guys charging in through the door, and like I thought, they were all sprinting past Boone and me and tearing around the corner to get to the cells.

Boone and I ran through the front door and charged down the street to the livery. Boone split off to get the horses, and I ran into the livery stable. Richards was right where I left him. I reached down, grabbed the front of his shirt, and threw him over my shoulder. He made a few noises, but the gag I'd shoved into his mouth kept him from saying much.

I ran through the stable and threw Richards over the packhorse. The air whooshed out of him when he landed, and I made a fast job of tying his hands and feet under the horse's belly. We mounted and reined the horses around as men spilled out of the sheriff's office, framed in the light of their lanterns, shouting and moving in our direction.

I led the way out of town, drawing the pack horse up behind me. "Discourage 'em," I told Boone.

He lifted his Winchester and dusted the ground around them. Boone then lifted the rifle and planted a couple bullets in the frame of the sheriff's office and jail, just to be thorough. They skidded to a stop, cursing and shaking their fists, but they weren't moving forward anymore, not when they were still standing in the light and staring toward us in the darkness.

I put my heels to my horse, and we left Kerrville in a hurry. The first stop would be made to move Richards and tie him down, straddling the horse, once we were sure there wasn't any pursuit coming our way. The next stop would be the Fredericksburg jail, where I planned to have a few more guns backing me up.

CHAPTER 2

TRANSPORT TROUBLES

I had ridden the trail back to Fredericksburg many times, but never at any time with a prisoner tied upside down over a horse and vigilante gang full of whiskey maybe coming down the trail behind me. The bends and landmarks so familiar in daylight all looked strange with only a half-moon overhead to guide me.

I lifted a hand to call a halt after about ten minutes on the trail. Richards's moans, coming from behind me on the packhorse, were getting weaker as we went. I figured I had bounced him on his belly just about as much as he could take.

Boone closed up behind me, looked at Abe Richards, laying over the packhorse, then reached down and pulled a double-barreled shotgun from his saddle. He took a few steps behind us to the side of the trail and knelt down behind a mesquite tree.

"Got ya covered," Boone murmured. "I can hold 'em off for a while, if they're comin', with old Betsy here, but don't waste no time making that varmint comfortable."

That sounded like good advice to me. I approached

the packhorse, not sure for a moment if Richards was still conscious. He moved and moaned after I prodded him with my gun. After cutting the rope binding his hands to his feet, I hauled him off the pack horse.

He staggered on his feet, but stayed upright. I was going to have to cut the ropes around his hands and feet in order to lay him face down on the packhorse. I cut the one binding his hands and got a little surprise.

Richards wasn't as weak as he was letting on. When I cut the rope tying his hands, he wheeled around and swung a wide, looping hook at my head. I could have told him that was a mistake, only he didn't ask.

I sidestepped the swing and stepped in, lifting my right fist to his jaw. He was overbalanced, trying to come at me, and he fell face down like a sack of potatoes when I landed the punch.

Boone chuckled without turning around. "I know that sound," he commented. "That was the sound of your right fist landing on somebody's face. Sounds like that old boy's gonna be eatin' scrambled eggs for a few days."

"I reckon," I agreed. "Maybe he can mix in some applesauce to go with it."

Richards had actually made my job easier, seeing as he was out cold. I tossed him face down over the pack-horse and tied his hands under the horse's neck. Then I cut the rope holding his feet and retied them, with the rope going under the horse's belly to hold him in place. Once I had him trussed up like a side of beef, I told Boone it was time to go.

"Hear anything out there?" I asked Boone.

"Naw," he answered. "My guess is they went to the saloon an' called it a day. Them posses don't much like it when somebody shoots back."

I slowed the pace a mite when we struck the trail again. It was hard enough for me to stay on the trail, and I knew it like the back of my hand. That bunch we'd left behind at the jail, considerin' the amount of rotgut whiskey they had in them, would never catch us.

We reached Fredericksburg in the wee hours of the morning. Boone and I took turns catching a little sleep on the floor of the sheriff's office with Richards in a cell, rubbing his jaw and cussin' at me. No gratitude if you ask me, considering I'd saved him from a necktie party back there.

———

I thought I could smell coffee. I opened one eye and saw nothing but the back wall of the jailhouse. I was lying on the floor, looking through the bars of a cell at the back wall. I could hear Richards snoring in the cell, which was a lot better than moaning and cussin' me, which is what he'd been doing most of the night.

I rolled over and saw Boone standing there, holding out a cup of coffee. "Did you make that coffee?" I asked suspiciously.

"Take it or leave it," Boone growled, handing over the coffee. "You want somethin' better, you'll have to find yoreself a rest-too-rant."

I took the coffee, pushed myself to my feet, and trailed behind Boone out to the office out front. I slumped into my chair and propped my feet up on the desk.

"Anything happen while you had the watch?" I asked.

Boone shook his head and fished around in his saddlebag for some jerky. "Nuthin'" he said. "I told you those boys wouldn't do nuthin' but go to a saloon and brag about how brave they are."

I nodded and pushed myself back from the desk. "I'm going to send a telegram to the Rangers in Austin," I told Boone. "Keep an eye on things until I get back."

Boone nodded and took my place in the chair. I pushed through the front door and started down toward the telegraph office, trying to remember the name of the Texas Ranger I had met in Austin a year ago, when Leander McNelly and I had gone down to investigate a train robbery.

What was the name of that officer? My brow wrinkled up as I climbed the steps to the telegraph office and stopped at the top. Santo? Brandon? Stanton—that was it. Trey Stanton. I walked into the office and composed a telegram.

> Have the sheriff of Bexar County in my jail in
> Fredericksburg. Name: Abe Richards. Stop.
> Pulled him out of Kerrville before the lynch
> Mob got him. Stop.
> Can I bring him to you? He may be running
> a ring of robbers around Kerrville. Stop.
> Jake McCabe.

I sent it to the attention of Trey Stanton and wandered off to the café to get some breakfast to take back for Boone and me. On the way back to the office, I checked back in to see if I got a fast answer to my telegram.

Much to my surprise, the telegraph clerk was holding a piece of paper out to me when I walked through the door. I unfolded the paper he gave me and read it:

Describe Richards.
Stanton.

I scribbled down a quick message and read it back to myself before handing it to the clerk. It read:

Sandy colored hair. Six feet. Triangular scar on
cheek.
McCabe.

I took the breakfast down to the office and tried not to watch while Boone gobbled it down. I thought I had bad manners until I'd watched Boone eat. I gathered the plates, took them back to the diner, then stopped at the telegraph office again. There was another message waiting.

Believe the man you captured is Slade Jenkins.
Stop.
Outlaw from Colorado, believed to have come to
Texas. Stop.
Coming your way with another officer. Leaving
this AM.
Meet me part way if you can. Stop.
Stanton.

I tossed the telegram onto my desk when I got back to the office. Boone picked it up and read it, his mouth moving while he read, like always. He put the message down and nodded. "Been done before," he observed.

I stopped and turned around. "What do you mean? What's been done before?"

Boone picked up his coffee cup and headed for a

refill. "Bein' an outlaw and a lawman at the same time," he observed. He walked back and plopped himself down on the edge of the desk.

"Like who," I asked, one eyebrow lifted in the air.

Boone shrugged. "Ever hear of Big Steve Long?" he asked. "Up Wyoming way?"

I shook my head and sat down to hear the story.

"Lawman up in Wyoming. Mighty quick with a gun, they say. Killed him something like thirteen men while he was taming a town up there. Folks figgered out later he was runnin' a gang of outlaws at the same time he was sheriff. Got strung up for it, just a few years back. You want me to come with you to meet Stanton?"

It took me a minute to figure out that Boone had asked a question at the end of that little story. I shook my head. "Naw, Stanton and somebody else will meet me part way. Nobody followed us from Kerrville. I'll truss him up good and tight. I'll be okay."

I moved around the office, gathering up some ammunition along with my Winchester and some more rope for tying up Richards, or Jenkins, or whatever his name was. I wondered where Boone came by all the stories he told. The thing is, I had a feeling Big Steve Long had really existed. I wondered if Abe Richards/Slade Jenkins was another outlaw turned lawman. Crooked lawman, that is.

———

I left Boone to keep an eye on things here in Fredericksburg because I was still worried about the posse from Kerrville showing up in town and causing trouble. As I trussed up Slade Jenkins—might as well call him by his real name—I was hearing Julia's voice in the back of my head, telling me to take Boone with me. I decided I needed Boone in town more this morning.

Jenkins was still barking at me this morning about his jaw, where I'd hit him, so I went down the street and talked Doc Reagan into coming back to the jail with me to take a look. I had to promise him that Boone wasn't the patient. I couldn't blame the doc for that. Boone is an all-day headache when he's laid up.

Reagan looked at Jenkins's jaw, hemmed and hawed a few times, then poked at it until Jenkins let out a yelp. Doc stood back and took one last look at him.

"It ain't broke," he announced, then told me I owed him fifty cents.

I paid up and Boone told the doc he was a crook. The two of 'em exchanged a few words while I rolled my eyes. After the doc left, I had Boone hold a gun on Jenkins while I trussed him up, loaded him on a horse with a saddle this time, and tied him in.

Stanton and the other Ranger were going to meet me on the trail, and he'd already started, so I hoped to hand off the prisoner and get home this evening. I asked Boone if he would ride out to the ranch later on and let Julia know.

Boone nodded slowly. "She ain't gonna like that, you goin' by yoreself," he reminded me.

I put a foot in the stirrup and swung up onto my horse Sherman. "She'll understand," I said. "Can't be helped today."

I struck the trail for Austin at a brisk pace. This shouldn't have been my problem in the first place, and I was eager to get rid of it.

———

Trey Stanton set up almost immediately after getting the telegram from McCabe. If the prisoner was Slade Jenkins, he was a dangerous man, with several murders chalked up to him in Denver City and around the hardrock mining camps that still operated after the Pike's Peak rush had mostly played out. Having a man like that pose as a sheriff was a dangerous thing.

Stanton took a young recruit named Newt Fisher with him for today's mission. It was a way to start breaking the kid in. Fisher was eager to join McNelly up north, but he was still a little too raw for that. McNelly had come back to town yesterday to recruit a few more men, but had turned Fisher down.

Stanton mounted up and turned to see Fisher riding up on a scrawny-looking mouse-colored mustang. Stanton swept his eyes back and forth doubtfully, but Fisher raised a hand in the air.

"He'll go all day, I promise," Fisher told him. "He's even got a surprising turn of speed if he needs it. You'll see."

Stanton shrugged and led the way west, following a trail he had taken several times now. He kept the pace brisk, hoping to meet up with McCabe in the early afternoon—time to get back with Jenkins and get him under lock and key before dark.

Mesquite trees and prickly pear shrubs gradually gave way to post oak trees and live oaks. The trail narrowed, but remained well-defined as they left Austin behind. Stanton remained in front, calling a halt every couple of hours when they found ponds or streams to water the horses.

Noon came and went, and Stanton cast a practiced eye overhead to estimate the time. He figured it was about two o'clock, which meant he hoped to meet up with McCabe soon.

An unusual noise in the trees ahead and to the left puzzled Stanton. He lifted a hand to stop Fisher, his eyes sweeping the shrubs and trees to his left. A woodpecker was pecking on a live oak tree over there, then it abruptly stopped pecking and darted away while Stanton was watching.

Instinctively, Stanton reined his horse off the trail, ducking and swinging his left leg over the saddle. "Take cover!" he shouted.

Two guns sounded from the trees. A bullet struck Stanton in the left leg, and he went down, rolling and crawling to the cover of trees. Newt Fisher wasn't so lucky. A rifle shot struck him full in the chest as he tried to dismount. He tumbled off the horse and landed heavily on the trail, making one feeble effort to rise. He fell back to the ground and lay there, his eyes staring blankly upward.

Stanton crawled into deeper cover. Waves of pain from his leg washed over him, but he drew his pistol and checked his belt. He had plenty of ammo if he could just stay conscious. After fifteen or twenty minutes, he felt sure they weren't coming after a wounded man in the bushes. That was a recipe for death.

Stanton looked around to take stock. Both horses had bolted. Fisher was dead—he hadn't moved or made a sound since he fell. Stanton tried to come up to a kneeling position, then sucked in a deep breath and collapsed back to the ground. He wasn't able to move out of here. He had to hope that McCabe would find him.

———

The trail was deserted except for us that morning. Now and then, I glanced back to make sure Jenkins was still back there. He was quiet now. Amazing what a gag in his mouth could do to keep him buttoned up.

Aside from a stop once in a while to water the horses and give Jenkins a swig from his canteen, we pushed on. For the last hour, I'd been a little uneasy. When I pulled out the gag to give Jenkins some water and a few bites of food, he'd said nothing, unlike last night and this morning. He'd been giving me an earful then.

Noon passed, and we pushed on. I was wondering when I would cross paths with Stanton when I heard two faint gunshots down the trail, out there in front of me. I reined in and listened, but heard nothing more. I twisted uneasily in my saddle. They could be hunters, but I didn't think so. Not this close to the trail.

I looked behind me. Jenkins just stared at me blankly. My gut told me he knew what this was about.

I pulled both horses off the trail, dismounted, and moved slowly forward, parallel to the trail. I wondered if they had bushwhacked Stanton and the other Ranger. Half an hour passed with little progress. I pulled up next to an oak tree, took a swig from my canteen, and wiped my bandana over my forehead.

We'd lost so much time I would never get home before dark now. I might have to make camp near the trail and return home in the morning. I shook my head, not liking that idea, when I saw a shadow, cast from behind, moving up on me. I whirled to face my attacker, but had only a brief glimpse of a gun barrel coming down toward me. There was a moment of pain when the gun connected with my skull, then things went blank.

———

The sound of a woodpecker hammering away at the tree above my head brought me around. I squinted overhead at the sun. I must have been out for at least a half hour, I figured. I pushed myself to a sitting position and checked my holster. They had taken the Colt.

I staggered to my feet, grabbing the tree trunk next to me and grabbing at my head until the throbbing subsided. I looked around me. There was no sign of Jenkins, of course. If he'd had a band of robbers over there around Kerrville, they were probably the ones who'd come to free him.

I shook my head at my own stupidity, then grabbed it while another wave of throbbing passed over me. I leaned against the post oak next to me and pondered what to do next. The gunshots I'd heard might well have been Stanton and his partner getting bushwhacked. Why hadn't they shot at me?

No time to worry about that now. One thing I had going for me—my horse, Sherman, wouldn't have wandered very far. We'd been through a lot together. I put my fingers to my lips and whistled sharply. With no gun, I could only hope it was Sherman who showed up.

I didn't have long to wait. I tensed as I heard some rustling in the brush, then Sherman popped out from under the trees and trotted up to me. After rubbing his muzzle, I reached around to pull my gun from the scabbard. My head might still be throbbing, but I was feeling better already.

I swung aboard Sherman and moved out in search of Stanton, holding to the tree line and brush at the side of the trail.

CHAPTER 3

TROUBLE IN THE CANYON

I found two sets of tracks within the first one hundred yards. There was one cut length of rope, then another at the side of the trail. I was sure those were the ropes I'd used to secure Jenkins's hands and feet, tying him on his horse. The two sets of tracks crossed the trail and disappeared into the brush on the other side.

I followed the partial hoofprints and bent twigs and brush for a short while, but I knew I was losing ground on these guys. They were moving a lot faster than I was. There was also the question of the gunshots I'd heard and what might have become of Stanton and the other Ranger.

I retraced my path back to the trail and proceeded east toward Austin, taking my time. I did not know whether Jenkins and his rescuer had circled around on me. About two miles down the trail, I saw another set of tracks. They were moving west, toward me, then left the trail and proceeded south. I wondered if this guy was joining up with the other two.

Moving over to where the tracks left the trail, I dismounted and squatted down to study the tracks. There was nothing there to help me—just a lone rider coming from Austin who left the trail and moved in the same direction as Jenkins and the other guy.

I stood and stared off to the south, then half-turned when I heard a rustle in the brushes and a faint voice.

"Let me see your hands."

I could barely hear whoever it was. The voice was weak. I slowly lifted my hands, glancing behind me at the Winchester in my saddle.

"Keep the hands up," came the voice from the brush. "Turn around and let me see your face."

He had the jump on me, so I did as he said, mentally measuring the distance to my Winchester and wishing I had the Colt on my hip.

"Hey!" I could hear relief in that voice now. "McCabe?"

"Stanton?" I lowered my hands and crossed the trail, moving to the voice. I found Stanton lying on his back, propped up against a tree trunk. There was a lot of blood on his pants leg, and I could see he was in some pain.

I kneeled and cut away the leg of his pants, splashing water on the gunshot wound to clean it up. I reached down and put his arm over my shoulder, lifting him up and moving him toward Sherman.

"We've got to get you on my horse and get you to a doctor," I told him. "We're closer to Fredericksburg than we are to Austin. I'll get you to our doctor there in Fredericksburg."

"Hold it." His voice was strained as I lifted him onto my horse. "He shot the Ranger I brought with me. Fisher.

He's just lying on the trail back there. We can't leave him for the buzzards."

I stared at him, knowing we couldn't get the three of us back to Fredericksburg in time to help Stanton with just one horse. I had nothing to dig a grave with. The look on Stanton's face told me he wasn't leaving without us doing one or the other.

I shrugged and turned east on the trail. We hadn't gone far when we found the body of Newt Fisher. Standing near him, grazing at the side of the trail, was a mouse-colored mustang.

"That's his horse," Stanton mumbled.

I made quick work of catching the mustang and loading Fisher on the horse. Stanton watched me, a sheen of sweat on his forehead. I finished tying down Fisher and came back to look at Stanton. He was pale as a sheet and wobbling a little in the saddle. I used his reins to loop his hands around the saddle horn.

I tied the horses together and led the way back home. It was getting dark when I stopped in front of Doc Reagan's office and half-carried Stanton inside. Then I left Newt Fisher to be buried and sent off a telegram to Austin before going home to Julia.

————

I woke up the next morning with an egg-sized lump on my skull. Julia hadn't said much, but I knew she had been right about taking Boone with me. I stayed down and stayed quiet until the throbbing in my head let up, then rode into town to check on Stanton.

Doc Reagan waved me in when I showed up at his office. Stanton, he told me, would heal up with no permanent effects. I walked in and sat next to him. He had bandages around the leg, and it was propped up in the air. He shrugged when I asked how he was doing and asked if I'd taken care of Fisher's body and funeral.

I nodded. "Not your fault," I told him. "You got bush-whacked. No way to see that coming."

Stanton stared at the bedcovers and said nothing. I squirmed in my chair, trying to think of something else to say. I heard footsteps behind and turned to see Leander McNelly walking into the room.

I stood to give him my chair, my mouth a little open in surprise. "I thought you were in the Palo Duro?"

McNally shook my hand, looking at Stanton. "I had to come back to get a few things lined up. Might be a sizable campaign up there." He sat down and glanced back up. "Can I come over and talk to you at the sheriff's office in a bit?"

I nodded and moved on, hoping McNelly would find something more helpful to say when he talked to Stanton than what I'd managed.

———

Forty-five minutes later, McNelly came in and plopped down in a chair next to the desk in my office. Boone dragged a chair over, and we both just leaned back, waiting to hear anything McNelly came to tell us.

He started by jerking a thumb over his shoulder toward Doc Reagan's office. "He blames himself," McNelly muttered softly. "No way he could have seen that one coming. You boys need to be careful, though. Jenkins sounds like a bad 'un and he had at least two helping him. Likely the same ones running the robberies around Kerrville."

McNelly lapsed into silence, then walked over to help himself at the coffeepot.

"What about Palo Duro Canyon?" I prompted him. "Stanton said you took some Rangers up there. You back for good?"

McNelly shook his head, took a sip of his coffee and made a face. "You've still got Boone makin' the coffee," he observed.

"You get used to it," I told him.

"Hmmphh." He set the coffee mug down and shook his head. "I'm not done up there," he said. "I got a couple more men and sent them up yesterday." He hesitated and glanced at me sideways. "I was kinda hoping you'd come with me," he said. He glanced sideways again. "Maybe Boone could hold down the fort here?"

I propped my boots up on the desk. "There's a couple of problems with that," I told him. "What about Jenkins and his outlaw gang? They might be skulkin' around here."

"Could be, but not likely," McNelly said. "He's most likely gonna clear out of here. You still got to be careful," he added, "but those boys are gonna want to go somewhere nobody knows about them." He took another sip of the coffee, made the same face, and set it back down.

"What's the other problem?" he asked. "You said there were a couple."

"Julia," I told him. "You'd have to convince her I'm needed that much up in Palo Duro. Enough that she'd give it her blessing. I made some promises when I married her. Promised I wouldn't go traipsing off chasin' outlaws again unless it was big-time serious."

McNelly slumped down in his chair a little. "That's a big order," he mused. "Can you give me a chance to talk some more? Talk to both of you, I mean."

I swung my feet down from the desk and nodded. "Come to dinner," I said. "She'll be glad to see you. Ike, too. We can talk then."

———

Dinner was over and we were on the porch at the big ranch house. Ike, my father-in-law, had stretched out in a swing at the back of the porch, his wooden leg stretched out in front of him. A gentle breeze swept across the porch. Julia and I sat hand-in-hand, waiting as McNelly sipped from his whiskey glass and set it down on the table beside him.

"How much do you know," he asked, "about the Palo Duro Canyon?"

We glanced at each other. "Not much," I answered. "It's a big canyon, up in North Texas. Neither of us have ever been there. I guess you're having some trouble with the Comanches."

McNelly shrugged. "Might be more trouble with Comancheros than with Comanches," he observed softly.

We both looked at him blankly.

"Folks who trade with the Comanches an' get mixed up in all sorts of things," he explained. "Some of 'em are just a nuisance, but others are some real salty outlaws, into robberies, kidnapping, even murder, some of 'em. We think there's a band of 'em operating up there in or near the canyon. Could be some real trouble. That's besides the Comanches, who are getting a little riled up, and some other folks wanting to settle in the canyon."

He took a sip and put the whiskey back down. "Can't say I blame the Comanches, wanting to protect that ground. It's been a safe, hidden place for years, but we can't have 'em on the warpath. And it would make a great place for cattle ranchers. Long, deep canyon, over one hundred miles. Narrow, too—you could post a couple guys at either end and not worry about the cows, except maybe for varmints."

McNelly heaved a sigh and reached for the whiskey again. "So, you got two sets of folks wantin' the same land really bad and a bunch of scoundrels trying to stir the pot for whatever it is they want. Bad mixture."

Julia was staring at the floor, not liking where this was going. "Who," I finally asked, "are these Comancheros? I mean, where did they come from?"

McNelly shrugged. "Usually, they're just a mixed bunch of freeloaders and troublemakers. That's probably what this bunch is. Some Indians, probably not Comanches, but maybe Kiowas or breeds who've scouted for the Army sometimes. They hate the Comanches. Could be some outlaws who've drifted north from Mexico. Others are just white folks who've drifted west, looking for easy money and not carin' how they get it."

I squeezed Julia's hand. "I—we owe you a lot, after that what happened last year," I said.

Julia lifted her eyes from the floor. "Yes, we do," she agreed.

"How many men do you have, and how bad is this?" I asked.

McNeely stood up and walked to the corner of the porch. "Right now, I've got ten men," he said. "They're all raw, though. New, all of 'em, at least for battle conditions. Got one man was a scout for the Army. The rest are mostly cowboys, looking for something different. Couple of 'em served in the Army for a few months. No battle experience among the bunch of 'em. Best I can do with these boys is try to guard the settlers. Three families, just itching to get their scalps lifted, moved in at the east entrance to the canyon."

He came back and sat down in his chair. "I need a battle-tested man, Jake," he admitted. "It's why I'm here."

I shifted uncomfortably in my chair. "What about the Army?" I asked. "Can they help?"

McNelly brightened a little for the first time. "Not much up there in North Texas," he said. "They won't send any help from anywhere down here. Got a small chance they'll send a little help from Fort Union, out in New Mexico."

That rang a bell. "Pike Hardy," I blurted. "The lieutenant that came with us to clean up the outlaw nest in No Man's Land last year. He was from Fort Union."

A small smile crossed McNelly's face. "He was," McNelly agreed. "I asked if they could send him out with a few men. That would give us, uh, me, a fighting chance."

Julia leaned over and whispered in my ear. "Help him, Jake. He helped us." She stood and walked into the house.

McNelly watched her go, then turned and looked at me, waiting.

I stood and walked over to help Ike get up from the swing, then turned around. "When do we need to leave for the canyon?" I asked.

Virgil Diehl sat in his expensive seat at the Maguire Opera House in San Francisco, watching *Hamlet* for the fourth time. He sat alone as usual, and he didn't find he liked the play any better than he had the first three times. It was just the place to be seen, here at the opera house. Why, he wondered, did all these guys have to die in the Shakespeare plays? He got up and joined the crowd leaving the theater. He was headed for the closest saloon and some whiskey, just like he'd done the first three times he'd watched *Hamlet.*

Reaching the nearest saloon, he tossed back a whiskey, feeling the burn go all the way down to his stomach. He knew they tossed a bar of soap in this stuff to *give it a bead*. He could taste the soap in this batch.

Diehl scanned the crowd, seeing just the usual bunch of low-lifes and drunks he usually saw in a bar. He scowled and ordered another whiskey, deciding he would push his stomach to the limit tonight.

Diehl had done well for himself in San Francisco, he couldn't argue with that. He'd arrived two years ago, just beating the law out of Texas. He had owned a ranch outside of a town called Fredericksburg. Well, the bank actually owned it, but since Diehl owned the county sheriff, the bank couldn't collect what he owed or kick him off the land.

That had all changed when a man named Jake McCabe had come to town. McCabe had cut down the gunhand hired by Diehl in a fight on Main Street. Diehl wouldn't have thought that was possible. McCabe had thoroughly whipped Diehl's thug in a fistfight, then defeated Diehl's crooked sheriff in an election.

Diehl slammed his whiskey glass down and swore

bitterly under his breath. He had a lot to settle with McCabe, and he would, maybe sooner than later.

The thing was, Diehl's gut told him it might be time to get out of San Francisco, and his gut was seldom wrong. He had made his living along a three-block stretch of Pacific Street, sometimes called the Barbary Coast. That area had a history going back over twenty years as a place where honest people didn't want to go.

The other thing was, the call of whiskey and women brought a lot of guys into that area. Most of them were just off a boat of some kind or another, looking to spend money, or make a fortune, or both, in this town.

Diehl had rolled into town two years ago, sized things up, and partnered with two people to make his money. The first guy was known simply as Boots, because he had a habit of knocking people down and putting his boots to them while they were down. The second guy was a man named MacPhail who owned a saloon called Pacific Suds, located in the Barbary Coast area.

The plan was pretty simple, and it was like a lot of other people were doing on the Barbary Coast. MacPhail got some of his customers falling down drunk in his place, and Diehl, with help from Boots, hauled them off and sold them to ship captains as mates on the next voyage, wherever that boat was headed. The captains got free crew members, and Diehl pocketed the money from the ship captains. He gave a bit to Boots and MacPhail, always lying about how much money he was collecting.

Diehl had good luck, particularly with the Chinese. They kept showing up in San Francisco, and who was going to miss them if they disappeared on any given night? Maybe they were even getting a free trip back to China, for all Diehl knew.

Lately, though, Diehl felt his time might be up for doing this sort of thing. For one, San Francisco had a habit of forming up vigilante gangs and hanging people. It had been a few years since the town stamped out a gang called the Sydney Ducks, but it hadn't turned out well for those guys when they did.

His next problem was actually the Chinese. They kept coming in, more and more of them. Now the town was about ten percent Chinese, and Diehl had a feeling they were banding together for protection. Most of them lived in a small section of town known as Chinatown, and Diehl was feeling outnumbered.

The last problem was other guys wanting in on his little piece of the pie. They were some really tough characters doing what he did, and they didn't really care for the competition. MacPhail had told him just this week he was feeling the heat from a couple of guys who announced they would now work The Pacific Suds, *recruiting* ships crews. MacPhail hadn't felt like he could say no, and he didn't think it was a good idea for Diehl either.

Diehl tossed a couple of coins on the bar and worked his way out of the saloon. He figured things might have settled down by now back in Texas. It was really the only other place he knew. Maybe Boots wouldn't mind joining him. He could find a use for Boots, even if Boots used his fists instead of a gun.

Diehl pushed open the batwing doors, dodged a couple of drunks, and started toward the rooming house where he lived. One thing was for sure, if he went back to Texas, he was going to take trains to get there. No chance he would smack the back of a horse all the way to Texas. That was for fools.

CHAPTER 4

SETTING THE STAGE

The Houston and Texas Central rail line was getting kinda familiar to me now. I had ridden it just a year ago on the way to settle a score with a gang operating out of No Man's Land, west of Indian Nation. Now, with the Rangers paying, it was a fast first leg of our trip up to the canyon.

McNelly filled me in on a few more details while we rode. He had left eight of his men watching the canyon, hoping to keep a lid on things, with the other two waiting for him in Ft. Worth. It was an eight to ten-day's ride between the two, so McNelly didn't expect to have any news when we got to Fort Worth.

I pressed him for more information about the Comanches. I'd had little dealing with them, but what I'd heard sounded like trouble if they got riled.

McNelly rubbed the back of his neck and stared out the train window. There wasn't much to see out there but grassland and some stands of oak trees, so I knew he was mainly just thinking things over.

"Maybe thirty or forty warriors," he said finally.

"They've got the women and children with them too, though, and the old folks. They'll fight to the last man if they think they're losing the canyon." He stopped and stared moodily out the window again. "Most of 'em have moved up to the Nation, but the ones that stayed in the canyon mean business. They've rallied around a chief named Black Hawk, who vows to never go to a reservation."

McNelly lapsed into silence. "What about Comancheros?" I prompted him. "You were talking about Comancheros stirring things up."

McNelly nodded. "Scouts are telling us the Comanches are equipped. Got 'em some rifles. Mostly old Sharps, but they might even have a new Winchester here and there. They didn't get 'em from fighting the Army and probably not from the settlers. That means they've been trading with Comancheros. Who knows what those guys want? They're out for themselves, that's for sure."

McNelly drifted off to sleep, and I left him alone, staring out the window and thinking things over. I had left Boone in charge of things, both at the sheriff's office and looking after my family in Fredericksburg. He was a tough old coot, and I didn't worry about him, except maybe if that crooked Sheriff Jenkins was still hanging around. I shifted uncomfortably in my seat and told myself not to think about that. Somewhere along the way, I drifted off to sleep myself.

I came to, when the train pulled into the station. McNelly tossed my bag to me when he saw me stirring, and we climbed down. After claiming our horses and putting them in a livery stable, McNelly told me he was going down to the telegraph office.

He pointed north at a building about a block away.

"Check us into the Metropolitan Hotel over there," he said. "You can ride the street cars around for a while if you want to see the town. I expect to be there in a couple of hours. Just watch out for Hell's Half Acre. Starts down around Tenth Street. A man can get into a heap of trouble over there."

Fifteen minutes later, I was looking out my hotel window. This was the biggest town I had been in—bigger than Austin, I figured. After a few minutes, I went down and got on a horse-drawn streetcar. After I'd ridden around for about an hour, I hopped off and went into a jewelry shop. I haggled with the guy behind the counter and finally came away with a brooch for Julia. I didn't ask what it was made out of. I figured if I could afford it, it wasn't diamonds.

McNelly was waiting in the lobby of the Metropolitan Hotel when I got back. He was grinning and waved a piece of paper at me as I walked in.

"Heard from Fort Union," he announced. "They're sending ten men. We'll meet 'em at the entrance of the canyon, up on the northwest side." He tucked the paper into his pocket, and his smile dimmed down a little. "Don't know who's gonna lead 'em out here," he said. "Hasn't been decided yet, I guess."

Two men came through the door, and McNelly introduced them as two of his Rangers. "Hart and Davidson," he said, waving at me and making introductions. We shook hands all around and took a seat in the corner of the lobby.

"Any news from the boys at the canyon?" McNelly asked. They both shook their heads.

"Didn't expect to," McNelly murmured. He glanced around the group. "Any reason we can't leave in the mornin'?" he asked. Nobody had a reason not to. McNelly stood and led the way out the door.

"Let's tie into a good dinner tonight," he said. "Trail food ain't gonna be near as good."

We filed out the door and moved across the street to a café. I had the funny feeling I was being watched and looked around me as we reached the café. I didn't see anybody I recognized. Still, I couldn't shake the feeling. After a minute, I shrugged and went inside.

———

Slade Jenkins was a man who could change plans when he had to. He was proud of that. It's how he stayed one jump ahead of the law. Hey, sometimes he was the law, sometimes he was the outlaw. Whatever kept him on the right side of the cell bars and made him some money. After that, he wasn't too choosy about what he did.

He was a little worried back there in the jail in Kerrville, he had to admit that. McCabe had done him a good turn, getting out of that spot. Once he got put in McCabe's jail in Fredericksburg, though, that changed things. If he wasn't wearing the badge anymore, then anybody wearing the badge became the enemy.

Then, on the trail to Austin, his boys Able, Baker and Charlie had been a little too quick on the draw. Those were the names he called them, anyway. Names were too much trouble. Still, he couldn't be too hard on them. Not right now, anyway. He needed a couple of guns behind him, and he just wanted to be free and on the move. With a dead Ranger back there and maybe two, he was going to have a lot of law on his trail.

After his boys shot the Rangers and he'd laid the

barrel of his Colt on McCabe's head, they had dug themselves in as far back in the brush as they could and
hunkered down for a day. When nobody showed, he had
led the way north to Waco and made camp just out of the
sight of the suspension bridge.

Squatting around a crackling fire, Jenkins stared at
his henchmen. It was time for him to have a plan. They
only stayed with him as long as there was money coming.
The problem was, he needed one of them to stay back
around Fredericksburg and Austin. If the law was
coming after him from one of those towns, he needed to
know. Kerrville, he wasn't worried about. They'd be too
busy picking themselves out a new sheriff.

Whoever stayed behind to watch his back might feel
cut out of things. He would have to be careful how he did
this. If you left an outlaw feeling cheated and cut out of
things, it would be a good way to get a bullet in the back
of the head. He should know. He'd done just that, a
couple years back down the trail.

Jenkins stared out into the darkness, thought about it,
and came to a decision. He took a long pull out of his
whiskey flask, tucked it away, and stood up. "Baker," he
said, pointing at the man he wanted, "come and talk to
me for a minute."

Baker, he figured, was the laziest and least greedy of
the bunch. Turning his back to the fire, Jenkins pulled a
wad of money out of his pocket and gave Baker one
hundred dollars. Baker barely blinked, hiding the money
as he put it in his pocket.

"I've got to go up north for a while," Jenkins
explained. "I need you to look for jobs we can do down
here when I get back. Banks and trains, think about
those. If you see something you can do on your own, do

it, just don't get caught. When we get back, I'll give you something extra for anything you scout out and set up."

Jenkins turned to go, then turned back. "If you get wind they're hunting for me, send me a telegram," he growled. "I'll need to know about that. Send it to Trevor Smith in Ft. Worth and have 'em deliver it to the White Elephant Saloon. I'll pay for it."

After Baker nodded, Jenkins turned and went back to the fire. He had no idea if he would ever return to this part of the state, but the money would keep Baker watching long enough for Jenkins to make his escape.

He needed to get away and hide out for a while. Where better, he figured, to hide out than in the middle of a pack of outlaws and thieves like himself? He wouldn't stand out in a place like that. And he knew of no better place to fit that description than Hell's Half Acre in Ft. Worth.

Returning to the fire, Jenkins told Able and Charlie they'd be heading to Ft. Worth. They could lie low and spend a little of their cash up there, he told them, and they'd keep their eyes open for the next place to rob. Able and Charlie looked at each other, then looked at Baker, who was stretching out in his bedroll. They shrugged and agreed.

———

Leaving at dawn the next morning, they held to back trails and stayed out of towns all the way north. Saloons, gambling, and whatever else they had in mind would have to wait until they reached Hell's Half Acre or Able and Charlie would answer to him.

Six days later, they reached Ft. Worth, moving

slowly and carefully. Jenkins led them to the White Elephant Saloon and paid for the first round, just to keep them happy. He moved over to one of the bartenders, a man he had known since the war. Money changed hands.

"If there's a telegram for Trevor Smith, that's me," Jenkins mumbled. "You can hold it for me?" The bartender nodded and washed another glass.

"Any, uh, business going on around here I might be interested in?" Jenkins asked, glancing around him in the saloon.

"What kinda business you thinkin' about?"

Jenkins shrugged. "Trains, stagecoaches, banks?"

The bartender kept washing and shook his head. "Ain't really heard much you'd want to think about." He nodded at the crowd in the saloon. "This bunch here is talkin' about that stuff all the time. None of 'em is much good at it. Doubt you'd want to deal with 'em." He set down a glass and leaned on the counter.

"Might be some cows and horses for the takin' though, if'n you played it right. You could drive 'em up the trail to Kansas and sell for a fat profit. Would keep you out of sight while you make some good money."

The bartender set a whiskey on the counter. "On the house," he said.

Jenkins downed the whiskey and set the glass back on the counter, thinking things over. "Where are these cows and horses?" he asked. "And just how easy would it be to take 'em?"

The bartender leaned on his elbows and stared through the batwing doors at the street when he answered. "You'd have to plan it pretty careful," he said. "Probly need somebody to put up some money, hire some troublemakers and take the bullets for you if there's any shootin'. Good money, though."

Jenkins wiped his mouth with his sleeve and pointed at his glass. "Tell me about it," he mumbled.

The bartender poured another whiskey and set it down on the counter. "Ever hear of the Palo Duro Canyon?" he asked.

Twenty minutes later, the story about settlers flush with horses and cattle, Comanches and some renegades with designs of their own sounded promising. The bartender promised to introduce him to a few other men later, men who would do whatever Jenkins would ask for the right price. He advised Jenkins not to be seen with these men around town.

―――――

After two long train rides with a dusty stagecoach trip in between, Diehl was about to change his mind on the idea of taking trains instead of horses. Standing outside the station in Ft. Worth, he swatted at the burning cinders on his sleeves and cursed while the train pulled out. He stared over at Boots, who had somehow slept most of the way, which served to double Diehl's anger.

The steady, unblinking stare he got from Boots set off a warning bell in Diehl's brain. If he decided to get rid of Boots, he would have to be sly about it. Settling his hat down a little farther on his head, Diehl swept a glance up and down the street, looking for a livery stable. The first order of business would be a horse, and the second would be whiskey.

It was a walk of only two blocks down from the station to a livery stable. Diehl sized up a sharp-eyed old man who slouched out to meet them. Diehl decided to go on the attack.

"I need a good horse and a saddle," he barked. "I won't pay more than a hunnerd dollars."

The old man shifted some tobacco in his mouth, leaned over and spit. He straightened up and pointed at a sway-backed old nag in the corner of the corral. "That'll buy you old Bert over there," he drawled. "He'll carry you where you wanna go. Not as fast as he used to be, though."

Diehl snorted loud enough to scare the horses. "I said I need a good horse," he shouted, leaning in.

The old man chewed on his tobacco and said nothing. Boots folded his arms and leaned back against the rails of the corral, pulling his hat down over his forehead.

After twenty minutes of waving his arms and shouting, Diehl finally paid one fifty for a sorrel and a beat-up old saddle. He paid the money and watched while Boots settled on a small gray mustang. The old man agreed to keep the horses for them until they came back to pick them up.

Diehl paused at the corral gate on his way out, feeling like he'd been beaten on the deal, but not sure what to do about it. "Where can I get a drink?" he growled.

The old man leaned over to spit again, then pointed down the street. "Take Houston Street down there for a few blocks," he mumbled. "When you git to Eleventh Street, you'll be in Hell's Half Acre. Plenty 'o places to get a snootful down there."

Diehl set the pace down Houston Street, then turned east, eventually pulling up outside a place called the White Elephant Saloon. He pushed through the doors with Boots behind him. There was a fistfight in progress, and a drunk cowboy stumbled past him and landed face down in the corner. There was the sound of a fist connecting with a jaw, and somebody else took out a table on his way down to the floor. This, Diehl decided, was more like it. Boots could do his dirty work for him if he got into a fight in this place.

Diehl glanced both ways before making his way over to the bar that ran down the side of the room. He ordered two whiskeys and pulled several gold coins out of his pocket, picking through them before placing twenty dollars on the bar. "Keep it comin'," he growled.

Diehl could feel eyes watching him and looked left after tossing down his first glass of a vile-tasting whiskey. Three men were standing there watching him. Two wore greasy buckskins and had double tied-down guns. The third wore denim pants and a bright red vest. He had one gun in a holster on his waist, angled inward for a cross draw. The dude in the red vest spoke.

"A man with a few dollars could make some good money around here," he ventured.

Diehl tossed down his second glass and ignored the dude. He tossed down his third drink and fiddled with his glass, waiting for the man to say something else. Boots eyed the two gunhands warily.

Finally, hearing nothing else, curiosity got the better of Diehl. He looked back over. The dude in the red vest was sipping a beer and waving at the bartender for another. When he saw Diehl watching him, he shrugged and picked up his next beer.

"Just saying," he drawled, "that a guy with a little money could make a lot more around here. You're not interested, that's okay with me. Somebody else will be."

Diehl watched him for a moment, then gave in to his curiosity again. "Right here in Ft. Worth? How?"

The stranger shook his head and took a long pull at his beer. "Nope, not right around here. Man could lose his stake in a hurry in Hell's Half Acre, though. Nope, the place I have in mind is a few days' ride from here. Place called Palo Duro Canyon. A man could come into a good herd of cows up there for almost nuthin', that's what I hear."

The stranger looked sideways again. He knew when he had a man hooked. He pointed at a table in the corner of the saloon. "Wanna talk about it? I'm buyin'."

Diehl stared at him for a long moment, then shrugged. "Stay here," he murmured to Boots, "but keep an eye out for me." Then, he followed the stranger in the red vest to a table in the corner of the room.

CHAPTER 5

MAKING A DEAL

Diehl eyed Jenkins warily but he listened, knowing he was being set up. That part he understood, and it didn't bother him. He was used to dealing with men who thought they could separate him from his money and walk away. Diehl considered himself an expert at turning the tables on such men.

He listened while Jenkins explained the situation. There was a huge canyon north and west of here called the Palo Duro Canyon. Diehl pretended not to have heard of it before. His story to Jenkins was that he came from California and had never been to Texas. The less Jenkins knew, the better.

He leaned forward when Jenkins began to talk about four settler families wanting to move their cattle into the canyon for grazing. They planned to bribe the Comanches with some cows, believing they could share the land. Diehl rolled a questioning eye at Jenkins, who only shrugged.

"Mebbe," he said mysteriously, "they've been told there are only eight or ten starving Injuns in there, and the rest have all gone to the Nation. These folks have upward of four hundred cows and a couple dozen horses among 'em."

Diehl made a mental note to find out who might have told the settlers that the Comanches were all but gone, but then let Jenkins move on.

"So," Jenkins continued. "There's a batch of, uh, businessmen who figger to trade with the Comanches, giving 'em knives and rifles, mainly. Some ammo and such. They only trade if that's the best way to make money."

Jenkins leaned forward to make his next point. "Here's where we can make some money. If somebody with a few coins in his pocket was to tell these, uh, businessmen that they could attack the Comanches in the canyon real sly-like and make the Injuns think the settlers done it, we could sit back and watch. An' then, if we could get the Comanches and the Comancheros, uh, businessmen to fight each other by picking off an Injun or two and pointin' the rest at the Comancheros, we could sit back and watch the fun, then help ourselves to the cows."

Jenkins stopped to polish off his whiskey, then leaned his elbows on the table to make sure Diehl was paying attention to the next part.

"Then, we could drive the cows up to Kansas and sell the cows, horses, and such for twenny-five or more apiece. For the cows, I mean. The horses would fetch a lot more."

Jenkins set back to see if Diehl could do the arithmetic in his head. He produced a pencil from behind his ear and shoved a piece of paper at Diehl. "I done the cipherin'," he announced proudly. "I think we could make almost five thousand apiece."

Diehl ignored the pencil and paper and stared at the wall while he took a long pull on his beer. He figured the take after a drive to Kansas might be more like eight thousand, and he had no intention of sharing it with Jenkins. He also knew that Jenkins had no intention of sharing with him. For that matter, he had no intention of playing nursemaid to a bunch of cows all the way to Kansas. He could sell them to somebody already making a drive. It could be worth his while.

The real question was whether this was worth doing before he went south to deal with McCabe. He took another swig of his beer and asked Jenkins the question he already knew the answer to.

"Sounds like you've got it all figured out," he said smoothly. "Why are you telling me about this?"

Jenkins looked down at his shoes, doing his best to look embarrassed. "The thing is, I'm a little short on cash," he mumbled. "Me and my boys would need a little help to hire the Comancheros."

Diehl nodded and stared at Jenkins for several seconds without blinking. "Let me think about it," he said abruptly. "I'm staying down the street. Meet me at the café across the street from the Metropolitan Hotel tomorrow morning. I'll give you an answer then."

He prodded Boots roughly on his way out of the White Elephant Saloon. He wanted to get out of this place in a hurry, but he didn't feel like walking through Hell's Half Acre without Boots clearing the way for him. Boots thumped down his beer glass reluctantly and followed.

Moving up Houston Street, Diehl felt relief as they left the rougher part of town behind them. They approached the Metropolitan Hotel, which is what the train conductor had recommended to him as a good place to stay in Ft. Worth. As they approached the hotel, four men left the building and crossed the street in front of them, moving toward a café.

Diehl threw out his arm to stop Boots, staring at the men in the street. He instinctively pulled his hat down lower over his forehead and stepped into the shadow of the Metropolitan Hotel. His mind told him his eyes must be playing tricks on him, but there was no doubt about it.

McCabe was a couple years older, and it had been a while since Diehl had seen the man, but he was looking at Jake McCabe, he was sure. What was McCabe doing in Ft. Worth?

———

Jenkins watched while Diehl left the saloon with his thug. Then he got up and crossed the room to see his bartender friend again. "Got me a fish on the line," he announced smugly. "When can I meet these friends of yours I don't wanna be seen with?"

The bartender waved at somebody across the room. Jenkins turned to see two men standing and moving toward them. Both had shaved heads except for a strip of longer hair running down the center of their heads. Both wore a greasy leather vest with no shirt. Jenkins stared for a moment, then waved at Able and Charlie to join him. The bartender opened a back door, and they all stepped into the alley behind the saloon.

Jenkins turned to face the two men. The bartender stepped back into the saloon without bothering to make any introductions. The taller of the two men with the shaved heads looked at Jenkins.

"What kin we do fer ya?" he asked. It slightly surprised Jenkins to hear the man speaking English.

Jenkins tried to cover his surprise. "You speak Eng... uh, where are you boys from?"

Both men laughed harshly. Jenkins recoiled a half step from the reek of the stale whiskey, then held his ground. Able and Charlie watched, their hands not far from their pistols.

"Yeah, we're white," the taller man growled. "That's what you really wanted to ask, ain't that right?" He chuckled. It made a growling sound low in his throat. "Sometimes it heps us do what we wanna do when folks think we're Injuns. What kin we do fer ya?" he asked again.

Jenkins cleared his throat and tried to gather up his thoughts. He needed to keep the upper hand in this deal, he told himself. He tried returning the stare from the two men. Don't look at the hair, he told himself.

"You boys heard of Palo Duro Canyon?" he asked, hoping he sounded like he didn't care about the answer.

The two men looked at each other. "Just come from there," the first one answered. "We got a few others, been out there with us." He fixed a stare on Jenkins, then Able, then Charlie. "What about the canyon? That where you need some hep?"

Jenkins paused, not sure whether he believed these guys had just been out there. He decided not to ask about that. "How many guys do you have?" he asked.

"Nine of us if'n you need us all. Depends on how much yore payin' and what we're asked to do. I know it don't look like we've kept our scalps, but we have an' we intend to go on keepin' em. What d'ya wanna do in the canyon? Steal some cows?"

Startled by the accurate guess, Jenkins stared at the man, who chuckled harshly again. Jenkins cleared his throat one more time, still trying to get the upper hand. "I want the Comanches and the settlers to get at each other's throats," he snapped. "I want 'em both to think the other one started it."

The other man hadn't blinked since they'd started talking, as far as Jenkins could tell. "Huh," came the answer. "Which side do you wanna win this thing?"

Jenkins didn't hesitate this time. "I want them both to lose," he mumbled.

The tall man stared back, his eyes narrowed. He fished in his pockets, took out a toothpick, and stuffed it in his mouth. "That would take all our boys," he said, poking around in his mouth with the toothpick. "Gonna cost you a lot of money. We might need a few beeves when we're done, too."

Jenkins shrugged. "I'm sure there's a few extra cows to go around. How much do you want?"

The two men looked at each other, then whispered back and forth. Jenkins crossed his arms, rocked on his heels, and waited. He wondered how much money Diehl had. How much of it would he spend?

The two stopped talking and turned back around to face Jenkins. The tall one took the toothpick out of his mouth and jammed it back into his pocket. "Gonna take all nine of us an' we'll be risking our hair," he observed. "Cost you five hunnerd, all of it upfront."

"Up front!" Jenkins barked. "How do I know you won't take my money and skedaddle?"

"You don't. You're gonna have to trust us," came the instant answer.

Jenkins looked behind him at Able and Charlie. Both

were staring at their boots. Jenkins turned back to face the two Comancheros. "I gotta talk to my partner," he informed them. "I can meet you here tomorrow, same time." He started to say he wanted to see the other seven men, but decided that was a bad idea.

The two men shrugged. The shorter one spoke for the first time. "Tomorrow," he agreed. They pushed past Jenkins and went back into the saloon.

————

Diehl changed plans on the spot and moved down the street, around the corner, and down several blocks to an older hotel, where he spent the night. He didn't want to run into McCabe just yet. By morning, he still didn't know if he wanted to take the settler's cows out in the canyon, but his curiosity about McCabe had grown. He decided to keep his meeting with Jenkins in the café across from the Metropolitan Hotel.

Not sure what he would do if he spotted McCabe, Diehl took Boots with him again when they walked down to the café for breakfast. He took a seat facing the door and ordered coffee while he waited. He grinned to himself. The seat facing the door was the gunfighter's seat. He was proud of the amount of work he'd done on his gunhand skills since he'd left Texas. There were a couple of dead men in California to prove it.

Diehl had gone through three cups of scalding sour coffee by the time Jenkins came in. Jenkins was alone and took a seat with his back to the door. Diehl glanced at the red-rimmed eyes and puffy face and wondered how much time Jenkins had spent in the saloon last night. Maybe he could use that to his advantage.

They both ordered food. Diehl banged his spoon around, stirring his coffee, then dropped the spoon on the table with a loud clatter. He grinned to himself when Jenkins winced and sucked in his breath. The man was in awful shape.

"Well?" Diehl asked loudly.

Jenkins glared back. "Well, what?" he growled. "I talked to some boys last night who can help us, if that's what you wanna know. Gonna cost a lot of money, though. Mebbe more than you got."

Diehl's temper flared at the challenge, then he forced himself to calm down. He started to reach for the spoon again, then decided not to aggravate Jenkins too much right now. He grabbed the coffee cup and settled for a loud slurp.

Food arrived, and Diehl said nothing while they thumped the plates down on the table. Diehl grinned to himself again when he saw Jenkins staring at the food with a sick expression on his face.

"How much money? What would they do for us?" he barked.

Jenkins winced again and glared at Diehl. "Five hunnerd," he said shortly. "They'll start a fight twixt the Injuns and the settlers an' make both of 'em think the other one started it. We'll sit back and take the cows and horses after they've shot each other up."

Diehl stared out the window. Five hundred was out of the question, but he could probably make Jenkins cough up some of it. Suddenly, the doors of the Metropolitan Hotel opened and Jake McCabe came out, along with another man. Both wore badges. Two more men joined them. They were the same four men he'd seen yesterday, and all wore badges. They mounted up and moved out.

Diehl stood suddenly. "I have to talk about this with... my friend here." He pointed at Boots, whose mouth was open with shock. Diehl motioned at him impatiently, and they both stepped outside. Boots was still staring.

Diehl moved around the corner, watching McCabe and the other men. They seemed to be headed west. The badges, Diehl had to figure, were Texas Ranger badges. He'd heard they were back together. He stared west, thinking. What were the chances McCabe was going to Palo Duro Canyon? That could make his job very easy...

Diehl spun around on his heel and marched back toward the café. "Come on," he barked at Boots impatiently.

Inside, Diehl sat down abruptly and leaned his elbows on the table. "I've only got three fifty to pay that rabble you talked to yesterday. You can put up the rest if you wanna do this. Up to you."

Jenkins stared at him through his reddened eyes. A vein in his forehead throbbed while he stared at Diehl. "A hunnerd from me, four from you," he demanded.

Diehl shook his head firmly. "Three fifty or nothing," he said. He started gulping down some more steak. Jenkins didn't seem to be able to watch.

"Okay, one fifty from me, the rest from you. I'll meetcha back here around noon." He got up and left, his food untouched. Boots reached over and helped himself.

We rode out of Ft. Worth early, but not as early as I'd expected. We hit the café across the street when it opened at daybreak, then stopped off at the general store to pick up some shells for a shotgun one of the boys was packing. After that, we moved out and struck the trail. I knew we'd be off at daybreak every day after this. We'd been told it would take eight to ten days, but we were hoping for the eight.

Moving through grasslands that got a little hillier and rockier as we went, we kept up a good pace, stopping only once to shoot a deer. We were traveling light on food. McNelly told us to watch out for rattlesnakes as we got closer. I was used to copperheads down around our ranch, but rattlesnakes are a little pushier. Downright mean, if you ask me.

I rode up alongside McNelly a time or two to ask him what we were gonna do when we got there. He thought it over for a while before he answered.

"First thing," he said, "is we gotta find those families that are settling in up there. We need to tell 'em the danger they are in and see if they'll rethink things. A lot depends on how much they're willing to listen. If we're dealin' with some hard heads who've already moved in, that'll make it harder for us."

He paused to take a swig out of his canteen. "Second thing," he said, "is we gotta show ourselves to the Comanches and their chief, Black Hawk. If he's as crafty as they say he is, he might pull in his horns a little when he sees us. Might make him a little more careful. That'll help. After that, we'll just have to see what happens. I'm hopin' the Army shows up by then."

I nodded and drifted back. McNelly seemed a little worried to me, and he was a man who'd seen it all. He was a man to ride the river with, and he didn't get worried over the little stuff. It was something to keep in mind.

Along about noon on the eighth day out, we started to

move in and out between some rocky cliffs, with mesquite trees, cottonwoods, and some native grasses growing around the cliffs. McNelly, in the lead, turned a corner and pulled up. I rode up beside him to look.

There were red rock cliffs shooting up on both sides of a valley. I stared at the cliffs. "Whaddya think?" I asked. "Are those things a thousand feet high?"

McNelly leaned over to spit, then looked at the cliffs again. "Little less, I'd say. Mebbe seven or eight hundred feet. Purty, ain't it?"

That it was. I sat there staring at the canyon, trying to think how I could describe it to Julia when I got back. Then I heard a rustling noise in front of me and around one of the rock walls. My hand dropped to my Colt, but McNelly put out a hand to stop me.

"It's probly my other men," he warned. "I told 'em to wait for us at the entrance. They should have a camp around here."

A couple minutes later, McNelly's other eight men rode around the corner, single file, moving slowly. Seven of them pulled up a short distance away while the eighth rode up and saluted McNelly.

"This is Carter," McNelly told me. "Carter, this is Sheriff McCabe. What can you tell me? Have you talked to the settlers?"

Carter's face twisted up into a frown. "I rode down there with one other man just a couple days ago," he answered. "Didn't tell 'em we're Rangers or how many others we've got. Just tryin' to have a friendly talk. Man who fancies hisself the leader is a guy named Oates. He's not friendly a'tall. Ordered us off with a shotgun."

McNelly nodded, resting his hands on the saddle

horn. "What about the Injuns?" he asked. "Any sign of them?"

"Yup." Carter pointed down the valley. "Down that way. Maybe twelve or thirteen miles. Counted twenty-four warriors. Got themselves a camp for the rest—women, kids, older folks. Another two or three miles, I'd say. They know these settlers are here, that'd be my guess."

McNelly sighed and looked around at his men. "You boys stay here," he said. "I'll go down there with Carter and McCabe and try to talk some sense into 'em."

We rounded the base of a couple more cliffs and saw a circle of wagons in the valley. I counted five of them. We hadn't come within a hundred yards of them when a red-haired man with the longest beard I'd ever seen jumped on his horse and galloped toward us, waving a shotgun in the air.

"This here's private land," he shouted. "Git offa our land or we'll open fire!" Behind him, I saw three more men mount up and move toward us, aiming rifles in our direction.

CHAPTER 6

A BAD START

The sound of Oates cocking his shotgun echoed off the canyon walls. "Git off our land," he repeated. He centered the shotgun on McNelly's chest.

"We're Texas Rangers," McNelly said evenly, pointing to the badge on his chest. "We won't be leaving this land."

Oates blinked two or three times, his eyes fixed on our badges, one by one. "We've still got ya outnumbered, four to three," he rasped, "and we've got our guns on you."

"What makes you think there's only three of us?" McNelly asked. "You don't think I showed my hand up front, do you?"

Oates's eyes wandered from one of us to the other, then stopped on Carter. "You was here a couple days ago," he said accusingly.

"That's right, I was," Carter agreed. "You don't see the other guy that was with me, do you?"

Oates's eyes moved to McNelly and me, then back to

McNelly. He looked uncertain for the first time, his eyes scanning the rocks and brush behind us.

"You won't see 'em back there, but if you open up with that shotgun, it'll be the last thing you do." McNelly swung his eyes left and right to the men behind Oates. "Same thing goes for you boys," he said. "Lower those rifles and back off."

The three men behind Oates did what they were told. Oates risked a glance behind him and saw he was alone. Fear showed in his eyes for the first time, but he kept the shotgun aimed at McNelly. I slid my hand slowly toward my Colt. Oates looked at the rocks behind us again, and when he looked back, I had him covered.

"Drop the shotgun," I told him. "It's time to have a talk."

Oates wheeled his horse around and motioned over his shoulder, riding toward the wagons parked farther down into the canyon. He dismounted and seated himself on a log which had been drawn up to one side of the fire. He pointed at a log on the other side. McNelly, Carter, and I sat down. The other settlers stood behind Oates. They still held their rifles, but they pointed them down at the ground. Behind them, I could hear the cattle. They had them spread out to the north wall of the canyon, most likely.

Oates put his shotgun on the ground at his feet and glared at McNelly, crossing his arms over his chest. "Tell me why you're here," he growled.

"Injuns," McNelly said shortly. "Bunch of 'em down the canyon, there. They ain't likely to take kindly to you movin' in here and settin' up shop among 'em."

Oates stared at McNelly. I could see in his eyes he didn't believe it. "How many?" he challenged. "Where?"

Carter spoke. "'Bout two dozen I seen off thataway." He pointed north and west, down the canyon.

"You're a liar!" The words burst out of Oates, and I saw Carter's hand drop toward his pistol. McNelly reached over and stopped him.

"Where you from, Oates?" he rasped.

"Ohio." Oates left off glaring at Carter and went back to glaring at McNelly.

"I'll give you a little free advice about living down here," McNelly said smoothly. "In Texas, if you call a man a liar, you better be prepared to back it up with a gun. Otherwise, it's the best way I know to get a bellyful of lead."

Oates glanced down at his shotgun, and his hand moved ever so slowly toward it. I dropped my right hand down and rested it on the butt of my Colt. Oates saw it. His hand stopped moving, and he looked sideways at me. I could see fear on his face. He'd seen how fast I covered him last time.

Oates sat back on the log, a red blush climbing up his neck and into his cheeks. "Git out," he snarled. "We don't need you around here."

McNelly shrugged and stood. Carter and I did the same, then turned and mounted up. Oates stood stiffly near the fire, watching us ride out. When we reached the mouth of the canyon, we heard hoofbeats. We wheeled around, ready for the worst.

One of the settlers emerged from behind a rocky face and rode up slowly. He removed his hat and spoke to McNelly.

"Captain," he said slowly. "Oates don't speak for all of us. My name is Williams—Dan Williams. I'm here with my family—my wife and my little girl. I need them other settlers to make a go of it here, and I don't wanna cross Oates. My wife and me would appreciate it though, if you and your men would stay awhile and keep an eye on us."

McNelly reached out and shook Williams's hand. "We'll stay awhile," he agreed. "Oates doesn't deserve it, but we'll even keep an eye out to save his scalp." He looked over Williams's shoulder and thought for a moment.

"Do me a favor," he told Williams, who nodded and waited.

"Get them to form those wagons into a circle. Better yet, you don't have many wagons, so make a half circle up against the canyon wall. Easier to defend."

"That would leave the cattle unguarded," Williams protested. "Oates and the others ain't never gonna do that."

"If they get to the cattle, they'll take a few. Not all of 'em by any means. Not the Comanches, anyway. You let them have a few to eat, you might be able to live with 'em peaceful. And you'll be alive. You tell Oates and the others. We can help round 'em up if they get run off."

"I'll tell 'em." Williams turned and rode back to his camp while we continued out of the canyon to rejoin the other nine men who gathered around us.

"Mostly they're not listening," McNelly said grimly.

"What now, Cap'n?" asked one of the men.

"Now," McNelly said, "we got to go check on the Comanches. We need to know what they're going to do about these settlers."

———

We left at daybreak the next morning, figuring on taking most of the day to reach the northern rim of the canyon and scout a spot to watch the Comanches. We didn't have enough men to show ourselves and warn them off. Or as McNelly said:

"If we had the boys from the Army here, and threw in a few settlers to help out, we'd have about even firepower with 'em. As it is, I'm hoping to keep things quiet until I get some reinforcements."

I asked him to fill me in a little more on Black Hawk, the Comanche chief, and how much he thought the Army might do if others joined Black Hawk and a war broke out with settlers. Having seen the canyon, I felt sure more cattle and people were going to follow these.

McNelly tilted his hat forward and squinted into the rising sun. "Black Hawk is a smart man, from what I've heard. I don't think he'll want to start an all-out war with the pony soldiers. They're trying to hang on to what they see as their rightful land. Sooner or later, though, push is gonna come to shove. I just hope it doesn't happen right now, on my watch."

I rode along, wondering about the soldiers coming from Fort Union. Did McNelly think there might be more coming after those?

McNelly shook his head. "Not right now, from what I hear. Grant has made some noises about sending Phil Sheridan back in here, though. He'd be on the attack if he came in, just like he was a few years ago. Right now, though, Sheridan has his hands full with governors, judges and such that don't want to go along with reconstruction. If he clears his plate and Grant sends him in, it's gonna be a big dust-up for sure."

We worked our way along the north side of the

canyon. Morning rays of sun lit up the red rock faces on the far side, then later, the greenery on the canyon floor showed. I moved along, enjoying the creak of the saddle leather and wondering how long things could stay this peaceful.

I glanced back at the mouth of the canyon, and I realized how narrow it was. A cattle owner could post a couple of cowboys at the entrance and keep the cows in. If the other canyon mouth looked like this one, you could keep the cows penned up and grazing with just a few hands. Being a small-time cattle owner myself, I knew what a good deal this would be.

It struck me that a big cattle owner might have his eye on this place. He might just drive out these small settlers, I thought. I asked McNelly what he thought about that.

He nodded grimly. "I expect you can count on that," he answered. "I'd be surprised if Goodnight don't have his eye on this place already. That's another thing that could blow up around here. Big cattleman versus settlers versus Comanches. That might take some serious troops to settle things down."

———

It was in the mid-afternoon when Carter came back from scouting near the rim and motioned to McNelly. They talked in low tones, then McNelly turned and waved his arm at the rest of us. "Carter's spotted a warrior camp across on the other side of the canyon. We're gonna dismount here and move up on foot for a better look. Keep yore heads down—don't skylight yourself. Those Comanches got some sharp eyes."

We ground-hitched our horses and walked forward,

covering the last ten yards on our bellies. I peered over the edge and saw some teepees, warriors, and horses. They at least didn't look like they were forming up a war party. No war paint, no mounting up all the warriors. They were scattered about, skinning deer, eating, or sleeping in the shade.

McNelly poked my arm and pointed to the side of one teepee. There were rifles stacked there, I was guessing there was one for each man. I shook my head. If they had ammo, they were well-armed. I swept my eyes from left to right, counting. Looked like Carter was right. I figured about twenty-five of them.

McNelly gave a hand signal, and we crawled back away from the ledge. We gathered around him, holding onto our horse's reins and waiting while he thought about what he'd just seen. After a while, he turned and faced us.

"At least they're not forming up for a raid, far as I can see," he said. "Anybody disagree with that?" We all shook our heads, and McNelly nodded. "Let's hope it stays that way for a while," he muttered. "Let's ride back, keep an eye on the settlers, and wait for the soldiers."

Lieutenant Pike Hardy had a decision to make, and he needed to make it pretty soon. He needed to decide whether to stay in the Army. He could muster out in about one month, or he could re-up. He had assumed for the last few years that he would stay in the Army for life, but now he wasn't so sure.

He had always thought of the Army as his family and his life. Coming from the background he did, that wasn't surprising, he knew that. He didn't talk much about his childhood. Mostly, he tried to forget about it. The Army helped him do that. Lately, though, he had felt the need to stop running. Running from his past. He'd found out that running didn't work.

People seemed to take it for granted that Pike Hardy knew his way around northwestern Texas and eastern New Mexico so well. They figured he had just learned it when he led expeditions against outlaws in No Man's Land and the occasional Comanche uprising. The fact was, Pike Hardy knew the land so well, and in particular, knew the Comanches so well because he had been one of them.

His memories were vague. His family had settled and started farming in Texas. He wasn't exactly sure where it had been, but he thought it was in north Central Texas. One morning, the Comanches had come. They had killed his mother and father, and the Indians had taken him and his sister with them.

He was small, so the Comanches had taken care of him, teaching him tracking and hunting skills. They had moved frequently, and he lost track of where they were, but he felt sure they had drifted south for several years.

The Comanches began taking him with them on raids, taking cattle and killing settlers. One day, they took him down into Mexico for a raid. They had taken the farmer's cattle, killed the husband and wife, and had taken a girl captive. She was a little older than Pike. Her name, he remembered, was Maria. They had come back across the Rio Grande into the United States, bringing Maria with them.

On the way home, Pike had come down with small-pox. It was a disease greatly feared by the Comanches.

Many had died from it. The raiding party left Pike behind, and they had left Maria to care for him. Maria had nursed him back to health, and he had returned her to her village after he recovered.

Afterward, he had returned to the States, drifting north and east, raiding farms to steal his food. He'd become very good at that. When the war started, he lied about his age and joined the Union Army. He didn't want to remember his past, so he changed his last name, calling himself Pike Hardy.

Hardy had found a home here at Fort Union. It had fallen to him to patrol No Man's Land, Northeastern New Mexico and Northwestern Texas. The fact that the land was still somewhat familiar to him helped. Beyond that, he just enjoyed bringing law to an untamed land.

He had raided an outlaw fort in No Man's Land last year, working with a Texas Ranger named McNelly and a sheriff named McCabe. A small smile crossed Hardy's face as he thought about that assignment. It was the one he was proudest of, and it had started him thinking maybe there was something he wanted to do beyond the Army.

The sound of Cookie banging a spoon on a metal pot startled him back to the present and told him it was time for grub. Cookie was what passed for a cook in their outfit. His stomach had almost gotten used to it. Hardy hopped down from the wall where he'd been sitting and joined the line. He made up his mind that he would inform his commanding officer about his decision by the end of the week.

———

Vince Cable sat down heavily on a bench outside the telegraph office in Fredericksburg, Texas, partly puzzled and partly angry. He had to admit to himself that the angry part was more and more what he was feeling lately.

Cable, who had gotten used to Slade Jenkins calling him Baker, had been left behind while Jenkins and the other two from the gang went north to check on something. Jenkins had assured him he wasn't being left behind, as his was the important job of studying out and setting up the jobs they would all do when Jenkins came back.

Cable let out an angry snort and stared moodily at the telegraph office. The deal had been that he would watch McCabe and make sure he wasn't getting a posse together, or calling in the Rangers to chase Jenkins. Also, he could scout any good jobs they could pull off when the gang got back.

Cable had done his job. He'd started by watching the sheriff's office in Fredericksburg. The first couple of days he hadn't seen McCabe at all, but that didn't seem too unusual. A sheriff had to cover the whole county, so maybe McCabe was just out on the road somewhere. An old coot with a badge usually covered the sheriff's office, probably the deputy.

On the third day, even the deputy hadn't shown up. Just a guy with a wooden leg. That's when Cable started thinking Jenkins needed to be notified. First of all, the fact that McCabe didn't seem to be around might mean he was out hunting Jenkins, something his boss wanted to know about.

The other thing was that Fredericksburg seemed ripe for a couple of robberies. The old deputy had some bark on him, Cable was sure of that, but he felt he could take the guy down. And if the deputy wasn't around on some days, that just left the guy with a wooden leg. How tough would it be to rob the bank if the only law was one guy with a wooden leg?

Three days ago, he had sent a long telegraph to Jenkins. It went to Trevor Smith, to be delivered to the White Elephant Saloon in Ft. Worth, just like Jenkins had told him to do. Every morning for three days he had gone to the telegraph office, sure that he would find a quick reply from Jenkins. When that didn't happen, he had sent the telegram again yesterday. Still no answer.

Cable stayed on the bench for a while, stewing. He concluded it was time to look out for himself, whatever Jenkins might be doing. He was ignoring Cable, or else he was doing some jobs with the other boys and leaving Cable out of things. Either way, he decided, he was on his own now.

Leaving the bench, Cable decided his first act would be to scope out the First Bank of Fredericksburg. That looked like an excellent target. He walked three blocks and turned left, then crossed the street and entered the bank.

"Can I help you, sir?"

It startled Cable. He hadn't thought about what to do when he went inside, and the sudden question threw him off. His brain fumbled for an answer.

"I, uh, would like to open an account," he mumbled.

"Certainly, sir." The clerk took out a sheet of paper and picked up a pencil. "Name, please?"

That was another tough one. He couldn't give his real name, could he? "Sam Baker," he finally answered. Jenkins already called him Baker, and that was all that came to mind.

After making up a couple more lies, Cable stumbled through the rest of the application. The clerk wrote something and pushed the paper across the desk at Carter. "Just sign right there, sir, and your account will be open."

Cable picked up a pencil and marked an X where the clerk had pointed. Writing wasn't something he ever learned how to do.

The clerk raised an eyebrow just slightly, but then smiled and pushed the paper into a desk drawer. "Now then, sir, how much money would you like to deposit?"

Cable felt his ears burning and turning red. "Uh, I have...". He fumbled around in his pockets. "I have six bits." He pushed a dollar and a half across the desk.

Ten minutes later, Cable had made his escape from the bank. He was as embarrassed as he could remember being in a while. Well, maybe Mary Lou, a girl from his hometown, had embarrassed him that much one time.

Cable found a saloon just down the street and bellied up to a whiskey. Now, he was going to rob that bank just to get even.

CHAPTER 7

A WILD SHOT

Diehl was almost excited as they approached the canyon. He was sick and tired of the heat and dust, but there were tracks along the way that seemed to say McCabe was out there in front of him. Carlos, one of the Comancheros, rode out in front every couple of hours, and he paid a lot of attention to the tracks in front of them. The head Comanchero, a bald guy named Murphy, hadn't been inclined to talk much.

Diehl had solved that problem by giving Murphy his share of the money upfront, with a promise of a bonus at the end of the job. That had loosened the man's tongue a little. Still, he talked little. Once in a while, Jenkins saw Murphy talking to Diehl, and that made Jenkins suspicious. Had Diehl made an arrangement on the side?

Tired of being in the dark, Jenkins had cornered Murphy by the fire at dinner last night and demanded to know what Murphy knew about the party leaving those tracks out there. Murphy looked at him shrewdly, adjusting his straw hat on top of his mop of red hair, deciding what he wanted to say. Finally, Murphy motioned for Jenkins to step farther away.

"There's four of 'em out in front of us," Murphy said in low tones. "Almost a certain thing they're headed for the canyon, too. Don't make sense it's the law with just four people. I'm guessin' there's more of 'em out there waiting for these guys."

"Does Diehl know about this?" Jenkins tried to keep the irritation out of his voice, but Murphy's head came up suddenly. That confirmed Jenkins's suspicion that Murphy had made a side deal with Diehl.

Murphy's eyes narrowed, and he chewed a wad of tobacco slowly, working out in his head how much he wanted to say. "My deal with you was to keep you up to date on what I know. I just done that. Nuthin' in our deal about not talkin' to nobody else."

Jenkins growled in frustration, dug in his pocket, and came out with a twenty-dollar gold piece. "What's Diehl want to know about?" he asked, passing over the coin.

Murphy pocketed the coin smoothly. "He wants to know if it's the law up there," he murmured. "I done tole him the same thing I tole you—maybe, but it don't seem likely that's all of 'em." He turned to go, then felt the gold coin in his pocket and turned back. "Seems like he wants to know in partikler about a sheriff named McCabe." He walked over to the campfire and filled a plate.

Jenkins stood in the shadows, stunned at what he'd heard. How did Diehl know McCabe? What did he want from McCabe? And what was McCabe doing up here? After a few minutes, Jenkins went over and filled a plate for himself. This was something he needed to think on. There must be some way he could use it to his advantage.

When we returned from scouting the Comanche position, I was less on edge than I had been on the way up. A little part of me was hoping we could actually keep the lid on this place. If the settlers held to their little patch at the entrance, and assuming the main Comanche camp was farther west and north of the warrior camp, maybe they could share this place.

I rode ahead to join McNelly at the head of our party and asked him if he thought that was possible. McNelly scratched his beard and shrugged.

"Mebbe," he said. "Depends a lot on whether that fool Oates keeps his mouth shut and don't go pickin' fights. Might depend, too, on whether there's somebody else who's got somethin' to gain by stirring the pot around here."

I remembered we had talked about that a little. "Like who?" I asked.

McNelly tugged at his hat and stared ahead. "Mebbe a big cattleman that wants the whole place to himself. Mebbe somebody wants to clear the place out and steal the settler's cattle and goods."

I fell back behind him, moving in single file and watching our flank. This could be like fighting a ghost. There might be somebody out there who wanted to start a war. The biggest trouble was we wouldn't know who they were or where they were coming from.

Shadows were lengthening by the time we were ready to take the turn for the canyon's mouth. The slow, grinding pace and the creak of leather at the end of a long day had me a little drowsy.

As we reached the last turn, I could glance up the

canyon and get a quick look at the settler's wagons. They looked the same as they had when we left. I relaxed a little. Maybe we could all get out of this with our hair.

Too late, I heard a rattle of rocks off to my left and a bullet whined over my head. There was a shout and another shot, then we were off and running for cover. We pounded down into the valley and galloped into a recess in the rock wall just inside the entrance. I threw myself behind a rock and sighted down my Winchester in the growing evening dusk. When I saw motion and a horse appeared, I held my rifle just above the center of the horse's back and touched it off. There was a shout and a heavy thud, then there was nothing else to be seen or heard out there.

Jenkins and the Comancheros had watched from hiding, screened by rocks and cottonwood trees at the mouth of the canyon. All of them covered their horse's mouths with a bandana to prevent any noises that would warn the party passing by. McNelly rode in first, followed by McCabe. Jenkins counted eleven others behind them. Jenkins had to assume the men were Texas Rangers, and they had recruited McCabe to help. This changed nothing. The plan was still to start a war between the settlers and the Comanches, with the Rangers in between. Things were shaping up nicely.

Jenkins saw Diehl, in front of him and to the left, reach into his scabbard and lift his rifle. He laid it across his horse's back and sighted down the barrel. Not comprehending at first, Jenkins finally realized what was happening. He leaped forward and shoved Diehl just as the shot went off. Diehl fired again, wildly this time, but it was clear he had been aiming at McCabe. Jenkins took him to the ground, where they wrestled briefly before Jenkins knocked him cold with a punch to the jaw.

Answering shots came from the Rangers, and several men vaulted onto their horses to give chase. A rifle shot from the canyon took down the man in front. He fell to the ground, writhing and clutching his stomach.

The Comancheros retreated, seeing that the enemy had taken up a solid defensive position. The wounded man lay on the ground, still moaning. Murphy ran up to him, bent down, pulled out his Colt, and fired a single shot to the man's head. Murphy bent to take a closer look at the man. It was Able, one of Jenkins's men. Jenkins stared, open-mouthed, when Murphy returned.

"Better'n leavin' him out there gut-shot," Murphy explained, holstering his pistol. "That there is the worst way to go."

Jenkins turned away, his eyes growing large with rage as Diehl began to stir. He aimed a kick at Diehl's belly, which Diehl only partly deflected.

"Gonna bushwack a sheriff?" He shouted. "Get the whole Texas Rangers force after us? What's the matter with you?"

Murphy stepped in and held Jenkins back. "That was plumb stupid," he agreed. "I think I've got a way to sort this out."

Jenkins stood back and waited to hear what Murphy had in mind.

"Our plan, as I expect you'll all recall, is to shoot us a Comanche and make the Injuns think the settlers done it. We lead the Comanches back and start a war. That there is still a good plan. Now we know who's gonna have to shoot hisself a Comanche." He hoisted Diehl roughly to his feet. "This idiot here is gonna do it."

Murphy turned around and motioned at Carlos, the tracker. "Carlos here," he said to Diehl, "is gonna lead you up close to the warrior's camp. Then he's gonna leave you there. You shoot an Injun and skedaddle back here afore they can lift yore hair. If you make it back, you can rejoin us. Otherwise, we'll just let them have you an' we'll make us another plan." He stared long and hard at Diehl. "You won't like it if they git holt of you."

Diehl opened his mouth, then looked around at the group facing him. He pointed at Boots, the man he'd brought with him. Boots just looked at Murphy, who shook his head no. Diehl closed his mouth and followed Carlos when he swung aboard his horse and led the way toward the north side of the canyon.

———

Julia walked briskly down Main Street in Fredericksburg. She had a morning of errands and chores to complete before returning to the ranch. Her first stop would be the general store, where she needed to pick up some supplies for a project she had in mind. She found it best to stay busy when Jake was out of town and possibly in danger. It kept her mind busy.

As she passed in front of the bank, she glanced across the street and saw a man leaning against a storefront. He seemed to watch the bank intently. His hat was pulled down over his forehead, and a bandana partly covered his mouth. A second look told her there was sweat pouring down his cheeks and into the bandana.

Some things about Jake had become second nature to

her in the time she had known him. He observed people keenly and had a nose for when things didn't look right. Julia knew this didn't look right. Without breaking stride, she continued down the street, but her planned first stop had changed. She continued past the general store and walked down to the sheriff's office, where she knew she would find Boone.

Hurrying through the door, she found Boone slurping his first cup of coffee for the day. He jumped to his feet and pointed at a chair, then moved to pour her a cup. Julia stopped him, her voice urgent.

"Something's wrong at the bank, Boone. There's a guy across the street watching the bank, and he doesn't look right. I think he's going to rob it."

Boone wheeled and picked up his Winchester, rushing past Julia to the door. "Stay here," was all he said.

Boone jogged down the street, then skidded to a stop when a gunshot sounded from inside the bank. A man burst through the door, carrying a pistol and a burlap bag.

"Stop," Boone shouted, lifting the Winchester. The man turned and fired. Boone heard and felt a bullet buzzing past his left ear, but he managed to lift the rifle and trigger a shot. The outlaw fell face down in the dirt of Main Street.

The order to report to Captain Wilson's office took Pike Hardy by surprise. He had been avoiding the captain while he struggled with his decision. The truth was, he had about three days to go before he was going to have to re-up or tell the captain he wanted to muster out at the end of the month. He really wasn't much closer to his decision.

Hardy was doing one of his favorite things, which was to work on the maintenance of Napoleon, the old Civil War cannon they had entrusted to his unit. He grinned a little to himself when he thought about using Old Napoleon to bring down an outlaw hideout in No Man's Land last year. He dropped the rag he'd been using to wipe his hands and decided it was time to get in a little more practice with his old Navy Colt pistol. That might have to be his weapon of choice if he left the Army.

A private came rushing up to salute him, catching Hardy completely off guard. He returned the salute and waited to hear what this was about.

"Cap'n Wilson wants to see you, sir."

Hardy turned and began moving toward the captain's tiny little office in the corner of Fort Union. "Right," he said. "Did the captain say what this is about?"

The private fell behind as Hardy strode away. "Nossir," he answered. "Just said to get you over to his office. Just got a telegram of some kind."

A telegram, Hardy reflected, could mean just about anything. He hoped it was nothing that would cause the captain to push for his decision any sooner. He paused at the door, adjusted his uniform and checked for any grease from Old Napoleon, then rapped sharply at the door.

"Come in, Hardy!" boomed the voice from inside.

Pike Hardy stepped in, executed a smart salute, then took the chair Captain Wilson was pointing at.

"I'm not trying to force your decision, Lieutenant," Wilson said abruptly. "Something has come up and you're the best man for it. If you're not going to be in the

Army, I'll have to send someone else. Read this and let me know if you want the assignment or not. Not taking it won't mean you've chosen to muster out."

Hardy grabbed the telegram and scanned it quickly. The words Texas and McNelly jumped out at him, causing a little smile. He set the telegram back on Wilson's desk. "We don't know how long this assignment would take, do we, sir?"

Wilson shook his head heavily. "It all just depends on what you find when or if you get there. You know how this kind of thing goes." He glanced up to find Hardy staring thoughtfully out the window.

Hardy scanned the telegram one more time. "No mention of Jake McCabe," he mumbled.

"Who?" Wilson watched him sharply.

Hardy, who hadn't known the captain could hear him, waved his hand and returned the telegram again. "McCabe was a sheriff down in Central Texas," he explained. "He was with McNelly in No Man's Land. I just thought he might be at the canyon."

Wilson reached out, took the telegram, and stuffed it back into a desk drawer. "Take tonight to think if you want to, Lieutenant." Another thought struck him. "You could go out there and muster out at Fort Sill if you want to when your time is up. Leave your number two in command to bring the boys home. Just think about it."

By morning, Hardy was still struggling with the decision. This could determine the path his life would take from here on. He threw the covers on his bed aside, strapped on the Navy Colt, and walked out to a clearing in the trees near the camp. He had laid a log across the clearing, and he collected beer bottles from anywhere he could find them. They made for good practice.

Hardy set up four bottles across the log and retreated about fifteen yards. He drew his gun, aimed carefully, and shot down the four bottles in turn. Happy with that result, he went back to set up more bottles.

Pike had to admit, the captain's suggestion that he could take the assignment and muster out at Fort Sill had some appeal. He wouldn't just leave in the middle of the job, though, he would finish it before mustering out. Then, his number two could bring the men home.

It would make for an easier decision if he knew whether McCabe was coming. He felt sure McCabe would help him get a new start after the Army. Still, he could just ride down to Fredericksburg and find the man later.

Hardy retreated the same distance, facing four new bottles on the log. He tried drawing and firing immediately, one bottle at a time. Not so good this time, he thought with a frown. He'd hit only two bottles of the four, and one of those was just nicked on the edge. Hardy holstered the Navy Colt and started back toward the fort. He would keep on practicing until he was satisfied.

Stepping inside the gates of the fort, he saw Captain Wilson walking over to his office. Hardy watched for just a moment, then he knew, in his gut, he had made this decision. It was time to get the hard part over with.

Walking to the captain's door, he knocked sharply and entered when he heard an answering invitation. Wilson had paused at the edge of his desk, looking quizzically at Pike. Hardy snapped a crisp salute, then blurted out his decision.

"I want to take the assignment, sir, but then I want to muster out. I'd like to do that at Fort Sill, sir, but not until I have completed this mission."

Wilson's face showed sadness, but he stepped around his desk and smiled as he held out a hand to his lieutenant. "I thought you might, son," Wilson said, giving Hardy a firm handshake. "The Army is going to lose a good man, but I know you're going to do well for yourself."

Wilson walked back down around his desk and took a seat. "Pick eleven men to go with you, your choice," he said. "Brief them on the mission and prepare to depart in two days. That is all." He reached for a stack of papers on his desk and began reading.

It took Hardy a moment to realize he'd been dismissed. "Sir," he said, snapping off another salute. As he left the office and walked across to get some breakfast, he realized he was feeling relief that he had decided and would move on now.

———

The next morning, Pike Hardy had a surprise visit from one of the privates at Fort Union. Tom Hostler had come to Fort Union more than a year ago, a skinny kid with a huge, bobbing Adam's apple.

Hardy found out, though, that Hostler could work wonders with Old Napoleon, the cannon. Plus, he had chowed down on the Army food and put on some pounds, which Hardy hadn't thought was possible, considering the food.

Hostler approached him in the barracks, saluted, and said in hushed tones, "I have a request, sir."

Hardy waited for the request.

"Word is, sir," said Hostler, "you're taking some troops on a trip to Texas, and I want to volunteer."

Hardy stared at him. "How did you know?" he asked.

Hostler shrugged mysteriously. "Word gets around, sir."

Hardy grinned. "I'll take you up on it, Hostler. We won't be taking Old Napoleon, though."

Hostler came to attention. "I've been practicing with the Winchester, sir."

"Good," Hardy told him. "I'll add you to my list. Be prepared to leave as early as tomorrow morning."

CHAPTER 8

DIEHL'S DILEMMA

We were spread out under the canyon wall just above us, which gave us a little cover, but not enough. The canyon walls west of us rose considerably higher, and they were steeper. I pointed west, and McNelly nodded. The others followed me out. I didn't figure the attackers were eager to come at us right now, seeing as how one of them was probably dying back there.

McNelly and Carter covered our movement, and we found a new position about a half mile farther in. We took up positions in the shadow of the canyon wall, rolling rocks in to give us a firing position. McNelly and Carter joined us, with no more gunshots going off.

McNelly dismounted and moved over to join me, watching for movement as darkness fell. "Who do ya figger it was?" he asked.

I shrugged. "I don't think it was the Comanches," I said. "They wouldn't have given themselves away with one shot that missed. They made some noise, too, and besides that, they wouldn't have quit that easy. Even

Oates, over there with the settlers, ain't crazy enough to attack us. That means somebody else is out there."

"Yeah, that's what I figger too," he agreed. "Somebody that wants to stir up trouble. Can't think why they gave themselves away with that shot, though." He chewed his lip thoughtfully. "Gotta be somebody with something to gain, maybe stealing the settlers' cows. Maybe Comancheros. They'd take the cows and sell 'em to somebody driving to Kansas."

Darkness closed in on us. McNelly posted a rotating shift of four men to stay on watch, and we moved back to the canyon wall. "How are we fixed for supplies?" I asked.

McNelly shook his head. "Okay for food, probly four or five days' worth. Water not so good, though. Need water for the horses, too." He squatted on his heels and leaned back against the wall. "I might need to send Carter out to do a little scouting tonight."

"I grew up in the backwoods of Kentucky," I told him. "I can be downright sneaky out there at night if Carter needs some help."

McNelly stroked his chin thoughtfully, then shook his head. "I might need you here more'n I need you out there tonight," he said. "Let's see what Carter can find tonight, and then we'll see about tomorrow."

Diehl was startled when Carlos dismounted and motioned to him to do the same. Diehl swung down from his horse, then turned to Carlos.

"We just got started," he protested.

"Sshhh!" The command from Carlos was low and

urgent. Diehl lapsed into silence and watched warily as Carlos walked back to him.

"We go past the settler's camp now. I tell you when you can ride again. If you talk again before I tell you to talk, I will make it the last thing you do. The herd is out there, too. We go around the cows."

Diehl backed up against his horse's flank and nodded silently. He had a feeling Carlos wasn't just making an empty threat. For more than a mile, he followed Carlos on foot, leading his horse past the settler's encampment.

When Carlos gave the sign, he remounted, and they proceeded to the east face of the canyon. From there, they proceeded north.

Diehl knew they would probably reach the warrior camp tonight, a thought which helped him remain silent. He thought about what had happened tonight so far and cursed himself under his breath for being such a fool.

It had seemed so easy at the time. McCabe was riding past, looking the other way, just like all the other Rangers. Diehl could take him down with one shot, and there was no way the Rangers could do anything but get out from under the Comanchero guns.

Without McCabe, taking back his land should be easy. Just the old man with a wooden leg and his wife and that snip of a girl. Two boys too small to be a threat. Only McCabe had given them the strength to take his land and end that sweet setup at Fredericksburg. Without McCabe, it would be easy to take it back.

Diehl cursed again under his breath and kept plodding along behind Carlos. He would have to get sneakier about this. He wasn't used to doing his own shooting. He had to admit he was a little afraid of Jenkins and that Murphy guy. He would have to work behind their backs and be sneaky about it. Diehl's mood lifted a little. Sneaky was his best thing. He could do this, working his way.

For another two hours they walked the horses forward, the canyon wall on their right, their path lit only by a half-moon. Diehl had a feeling he might need to go back the same way. He looked for landmarks and constantly tried to get his bearings.

They turned southwest now. It was still dark, and they hadn't talked since before they passed the settler's camp. Diehl turned in his saddle from time to time, trying to commit the view of the north canyon walls to memory. He increasingly believed he would need to come back this way.

After an hour of moving southwest, they walked single file into a slight draw with a trickle of a stream passing through. Carlos dismounted to let his horse drink, and Diehl did the same. Carlos checked the moon overhead and swung his head from side to side, listening intently.

Finally, satisfied, he turned to Diehl and muttered under his breath. "Don't talk, just listen. I will lead us to a position south of the warrior camp. We reach that camp around daybreak, I think. We hide there. I mean, you hide there. I leave you there and leave a trail back to the settler camp."

"What am I..." Diehl stopped talking immediately when he saw the anger flash across Carlos's face. Carlos's hand dropped to the knife at his belt, and Diehl knew Carlos could slash his throat before he could ever clear the pistol.

Carlos waited, still glaring at Diehl. When nothing was said for another two minutes, Carlos continued.

"You will hide and I leave, giving them a small trail south to the settler camp. You wait until evening, then you sneak up and shoot a Comanche. Then you hide. Know where to hide. Leave no trail or they find you and kill you. Let them find my trail and follow me. You wait until they go. Then you go—that way—" He pointed back the way they had come.

Diehl nodded, glancing only briefly at the trail behind them.

"You follow that trail along the cliff when there is light. You will see a way to climb up the walls, out of canyon. Come back around canyon mouth, and join us."

Diehl nodded again. His brain had a thousand questions, but his brain also told him Carlos wasn't going to be taking any questions. Best to just hide in the spot where Carlos left him and find a way to sneak up close enough to the Comanches to take one of them down. He glanced at his horse, wondering how he would hide his horse, too.

"I show you where you hide and hide horse too. I know this canyon."

"Yes." It was the first and only word Diehl would say on the remainder of the entire trip. He just had to live through this. Then, he could start planning again.

Carlos led the way again, dismounting and leading the horse after thirty minutes. As morning sunbeams filtered through the clouds above the canyon, Carlos showed him a deep recess in the canyon face with a small open area behind it. He pointed.

"You hide here. Hide horse here. Go up on foot, one mile." He pointed north. "Then you come back, hide and let them follow me. I leave trail for them to follow." With nothing else said, Carlos mounted and rode slowly to the south, stopping once in a while to check the trail he was leaving. Diehl watched until he was out of sight, then led his horse into the recess in the canyon wall.

————

It was a hard five days from Fort Union to the Palo Duro Canyon, and Pike Hardy was frustrated with the delays in getting away. McNelly's telegram had said there were settlers at the southeast entrance to the canyon, which lengthened the trip a bit more. The southeast was the most distant entrance. For two days, he pushed the men hard, but these men were the best cavalry the fort had, with a spare horse apiece, so they kept up a good pace.

In the late afternoon, on the second day, they came to a suitable camping spot with running water nearby, so Hardy called an early halt. While the men set up camp, he followed the stream a short way into the trees and brought down a buck for dinner.

Hardy simply tossed the buck over his horse and brought it back to the camp, where his men took the carcass and immediately dressed it. After he laid out his bedroll and cared for his horse, it surprised Pike to see Hostler approaching again.

"Sir." Hostler saluted and waited to see if Hardy would talk to him before moving to the campfire.

"At ease. What's on your mind, Hostler?" Pike was curious about what Hostler had to say this time.

Hostler approached slowly. "Well, sir, they gave me my papers before we left. Free to leave the service, I mean. Cap'n says I'm free to go at any time, but I wanted to come on this mission."

Hardy stared, surprised by Hostler one more time.

"Why did you come, Private?" Hardy asked. "Do you want to leave us before we get to the canyon?"

"Oh no, sir, I want to see this mission through. Cap'n says I could talk to you about it. I'm from Jefferson, Texas, sir, out in the east part of the state." Hostler scuffed one boot in the dirt, trying to explain. "I wanted to come back to Texas, and I heard there were troops coming here. Makes it easier to come the first part of the way, but I'm gonna see this through. When you tell me we're done with this mission, sir, I plan to be on my way."

"Very well, Hostler. I'll let you know when we're done here. You can go at any time, it sounds like, but I'm glad to have you with us."

Hardy returned the salute and watched Hostler walk away, chuckling to himself at how similar their situations were.

————

Diehl stayed well hidden behind the recess in the canyon wall for hours. He was certain he had given Carlos all the time he required and then some, but the truth was, he was paralyzed with fear. Men had always done his dirty work for him. He promised himself one more time that's the way it would be again from now on.

Shadows began lengthening as the sunset closed in. The recess was well-shaded and cool, but there was sweat running down the back of his neck, and Diehl knew it wasn't from heat. He forced himself to emerge slowly from the recess. He had to do something now, or he would never have the nerve.

Diehl picked up his Winchester and double-checked the Colt in his belt, desperately hoping he wouldn't be close enough to any of them to use the Colt. He crept out from the recess in the canyon wall, staying as close to the wall as he could and moving from rock to rock in an effort to leave no tracks.

Carlos had told him the camp was one mile north, but Diehl didn't have a lot of confidence in that number. How did the guy know it wasn't two miles? Or maybe just around the next bend in the canyon wall? That second thought was scarier than the first one. After a few minutes, he realized it would soon be too dark to do anything today. Waiting another day was unthinkable, so he picked up his pace.

Off to his right, he could see the trail that Carlos had left to lead them back to the settlers. It was growing darker. That bait might just work, Diehl thought grimly, if he could get a shot off and beat them back to his hideout.

His hurry very nearly cost him his life. Rounding a bend in the wall, intent on what was in front of him, movement caught his eye. Diehl sunk down to his heels, turning his head slowly to the right, straining to see what had caught his attention. A lone warrior was riding in slowly from the canyon floor with a deer carcass slung across his horse.

As the brave turned north toward their camp, Diehl knew this would be the best chance he would get. He moved forward and crouched with a rock in front of him. The Comanche had his back to Diehl now, so Diehl wasn't worried about being seen. Laying the Winchester across the top of the rock, he sighted carefully, took a deep breath, then exhaled slowly as he squeezed the trigger. The warrior fell sideways and tumbled off his horse.

There was no time to lose now. If Carlos was right

about the distance to the camp, he was less than a half mile away, and they would have certainly heard that shot. Diehl grabbed the Winchester and started back, trying to stay on the rocks, jumping from rock to rock to hide his trail. He had gone only a few yards when he realized he needed to throw caution to the wind and run for the recess in the rocks. They would be coming on horseback, while he was on foot.

Diehl knew before too long that he had spent too much time in saloons out there in California, and his breath was coming in ragged gasps. He didn't dare waste the time to turn around and look. He just ran and dreaded the sound of approaching hoofbeats. At least, he reminded himself, they would stop to look at the warrior he had shot.

He had taken stock of some landmarks when he left to tell him when he was reaching the entrance to his hideout. When he was twenty or thirty yards away, he slowed and moved carefully, trying again to hide his tracks before turning in. When he finally reached the entrance, he ducked inside, stretched out full length on the ground, and eased his head back around the corner, looking for any sign of pursuit.

Staring into the growing gloom for several minutes, Diehl felt his stomach turn over when the shapes appeared silently, moving steadily and soundlessly. There was a brave in front following the tracks left by Carlos. The others were spread slightly behind him, following and scanning the ground in front. Others had their heads up, watching for attackers.

Diehl pulled his head inside, pushed himself up from the ground and catfooted his way back to his horse, hoping desperately his mount wouldn't whinny when the

Comanches pulled past him. He reached for the animal, pulled his bandana from his neck, and held it over the horse's muzzle. He pulled his Colt from the holster with his free hand and watched the entrance. If they came, he would get off a shot or two, but he would make sure the last shot was for himself. He'd heard all the stories about what the Comanches might do to prisoners.

For what seemed an eternity, Diehl stood there, frozen in place, not daring to move. It felt like an hour, but he was sure he stood there for at least twenty minutes. Finally, he knew he had to look. Would they have spotted his tracks and the recess? Would they wait in ambush? He had to find out.

Diehl walked the few yards to the entrance, not feeling that silence made much difference now. If they were still out there, waiting for him, he was dead. If they had gone on, he needed to get across the canyon, up to the rim, and back to the Comancheros.

Taking a deep breath and keeping a firm grip on the Colt, he stepped out of the recess and stood still, taking in what he could see. Darkness had set in, and he took his time, moving his head slowly from left to right and back again. He couldn't see them. He stayed there for a few minutes, listening to the night sounds, trying to pick out anything that didn't belong.

Diehl retreated into the recess and emerged with his horse. Now, he felt almost reckless. Death had passed him by, but he felt sure his number wasn't up tonight. The moonlight was enough to retrace his path across the valley. It was only a few miles, and he struck the trail along the opposite cliff wall without a problem.

Another forty-five minutes on the trail, and he had found the path Carlos had described, leading up the side of the canyon to the rim. Carlos had told him to wait for daylight, but Diehl didn't like the idea of being out there, moving along the side of the mountain where the Comanches might see him in the daylight. He dismounted and led his horse up, trusting the animal when he slowed to pick his way carefully up the trail.

When Diehl emerged on the rim, he felt satisfied he could stop. He led the horse away from the rim, hobbled him, and spread out a blanket on the ground. He laid on his back, clasped his hands behind his head, and stared up at the stars. Sleep wouldn't come tonight, but he could rest. He had earned that.

What would he do when he got back? Did he really want to rejoin Jenkins and Murphy? Maybe he would be better off staying in the shadows, looking for another shot at McCabe. Diehl turned those thoughts over in his mind while the knots gradually left his shoulders and the sick feeling in his stomach eased. At about four o'clock in the morning, he drifted off into a troubled sleep.

CHAPTER 9

TROUBLE BACK HOME

When the first gunshot boomed and echoed down the street, Julia grabbed the shotgun hanging on a rack in the sheriff's office and ran toward the bank. She rounded the corner and skidded to a stop, seeing the stranger who'd been watching the bank. He was down in the street, and he wasn't moving. She lifted her eyes to see Boone clutching his left arm, cradling his rifle and lurching toward the dead man.

Julia ran to put an arm around Boone, trying to steer him toward the doctor's office. Boone pushed her away, intent on reaching the man he had shot. "Got to finish this up," he growled.

"He's done, Boone," she insisted. She looked over to see a man clutching a small bag, now kneeling over the body in the street. "Look, there is Dr. Reagan, checking him over now," she said.

Reagan stood and motioned to two men to carry the body away. "He's dead, Boone," she explained. "The doc's coming over now to check you out."

Boone moaned loudly. "I'm done fer now," he declared.

Doc Reagan snorted. "Got yerself shot again, I see," Reagan growled. "Help me get him over to the office, Julia. Maybe I can patch him up one more time if he don't moan and whine too much."

Julia, long since used to the way these two talked to each other, put an arm around Boone and helped steer him toward the doctor's office. As she walked, she saw her brother Pete, who worked one day a week at the livery stable, standing over the corpse and staring as the two men carried the body away. He looked up to see Julia. His face looked strained.

Julia hovered in the doorway while the doctor cut away Boone's sleeve and took a closer look. "It ain't broke," he announced.

"Not unless you break it, yanking my arm around like that," Boone growled.

"Hmmph." Reagan stroked his mustache and walked past Julia on his way to get some supplies.

Julie trailed after him to a cabinet, where the doctor pulled out a bottle and some cloth to use for a bandage. "Is it bad?" she asked. "Does it just need to be kept clean and bandaged?"

"That's about it," Reagan agreed. "That, and you need to try to keep the old coot from moving it around. I'll put a sling on it. No telling if he keeps it on. Maybe his new wife will help with that."

"I'll get Alice," Julia promised. "I'll tell her what she said."

Julia walked back out to the street, looking around for her brother Pete. When she didn't see him, she walked around to the livery stable where he worked. She found him shoveling out a stall, still looking a little shaken.

"What is it, Pete?" she asked. "Did you know that guy Boone shot over there?"

Pete shook his head. "Didn't know him," he said. "I've seen before, though." He kept shoveling.

"Where?" Julia prompted. "Where did you see him before?"

"I seen him watching the ranch," Pete said. He stopped and leaned on his shovel. "I'm sure it was him."

Julia's first question, which was to ask if her brother was sure, died on her lips. He sounded certain. She blurted out the next two questions at once: "Where? When?"

"Two days ago. I was walkin' to the barn, and he was out there at the edge of the woods, behind the barn. I went on in and pulled out Pa's field glasses he had in the war. I came out and went around to the corner of the barn, laid down, and watched him around the corner. He stayed mebbe ten minutes and left. I been watchin' for him, but I ain't seen him since. Till now."

Julia nodded, staring out at the street. "I wish you'd told me," she said softly.

Pete shrugged. "Everybody's got stuff they're worried about already," he said defensively.

"You're worried about Jake coming back, Pa's worried about helping Boone and gettin' things done at the ranch, Boone's worried about watching the town until Jake gets back..." His voice trailed off.

"I was keepin' an eye out," he finished. "I would have said something if I'd seen him again."

Julia patted his shoulder absent-mindedly. The man, whoever he was, was dead now. She started down the street, then turned back. "He was alone, right? Are you sure there was nobody else out there?"

Pete nodded his head up and down several times. "I went out there and checked the tracks all around," he said firmly. "There was nobody else."

Julia nodded and walked to the general store. If the man was alone, then she wouldn't say anything. He certainly couldn't cause any trouble now.

———

McNelly called me over when Carter came in from scouting. I was judging it was around three o'clock in the morning, so he'd been out there most of the night. The two of them were sitting at the center of our small camp. McNelly handed Carter a steaming cup of coffee and sat down next to me. The hatful of fire we had used for dinner still had some hot ashes going.

"What about the settlers?" was McNelly's first question. "Did they take up a defensive position over there—half circle up against the canyon wall, like we told 'em?"

"They did," Carter nodded. "I crept up on 'em pretty easy, so whoever they've got posted on watch ain't that good at it, but they have themselves a good defensive position. They could hold off an attack for a while, anyway."

McNelly let out a brief grunt of satisfaction and leaned back a little. "And the Comancheros?" was his next question. "They've set up camp, probly, just a little outside the mouth of the canyon?"

"No, Cap'n, they've been moving tonight. They slipped back into the canyon and set up betwixt us and the settlers. Got one scout posted to keep an eye on us, out yonder, there." Carter pointed to the north. "Got one keepin' an eye on the settlers on t'other side, and seven camped in the canyon. Could hear a couple of 'em snorin' on my way in, I could."

McNelly and I exchanged glances. We hadn't expected this. "They're in between us and the settlers," McNelly repeated. He shook his head, trying to figure it out.

"You said seven," I reminded Carter. "Two on watch, but what happened to the other three? Where are those guys?"

"Well," Carter answered, "you done fetched one of 'em when you shot him in the brisket a while ago. They taken him out and buried him. That makes eleven. There's two more that went out by theirselves, past the settler's camp to the north wall. Then they turned west and north, following the far wall on the canyon. I didn't foller 'em most than a few hundred yards after that."

"Went north..." McNelly mumbled.

"Comanches," I said. "The Comanches are up there. You think they went to try to join up with Black Hawk? Could they do that?"

McNelly shook his head. "Nope. Black Hawk won't trust them that much. He might just turn on them. He might trade with them, but he won't trust them. They're more coyotes than fighters, anyway. That ain't it. It's something else."

"Maybe they just wanna rile 'em up, then," I suggested. "They somehow get the Comanches to come down here and attack the settlers. And us. They're camped in the middle to keep us from going to help the settlers. They take us by surprise when we try. They hope the settlers take out enough Comanches for them to steal the cows when all the dust settles."

McNelly slapped his thigh so hard I jumped. "That's it," he murmured. "That's gotta be it." He stood and paced around. "I'm hoping the soldiers get here in a day or two, but we can't just sit and wait for them." He turned around and looked at Carter again. "Tell me about the settlers' position. Right up against the wall, you said. How high is the canyon wall there?"

Carter closed his eyes, picturing and trying to remember. "Not too high right there, Cap'n. They're not that far into the canyon. I'd say mebbe thirty feet high, right above 'em, though. Real steep there."

"Hmmm." McNelly paced a little more, then had one more question for Carter:

"Could we get past that lookout they've got posted on us? Get past him, get out of the canyon, circle up above the settlers, and lay down fire from above?"

Carter's face slowly spread into a grin. "That there's a tinhorn out there watchin', Cap'n. If'n somebody was to sneak out there, fetch a rock up against his head and make him real sleepy for a while, we could surely get out."

"Do it." McNelly said crisply. "I'll get the men ready to move. Come back here and let me know when it's done."

I got my horse saddled up and listened at the edge of our camp. Once, I thought I heard a solid *thunk* out there, but it was probly my imagination. Carter came back in about thirty minutes, gave McNelly a nod, and we moved out. By morning, we were looking down from the canyon above the settler position, waiting and watching.

———

Jenkins got word by mid-morning that the scout Murphy had posted to keep an eye on the Rangers' camp had been attacked during the night. He had been standing at the edge of the Comanchero's camp, watching the Rangers through his field glasses, when two guys carried in the scout he had posted. There was a lump on his head the size of an egg and he spoke in short sentences, slurring his words so much it was hard to understand him. When Jenkins asked who had hit him, he only shrugged and stared at the ground, weaving back and forth on his feet.

Out of patience, Jenkins waved at his men to take the injured scout away, then turned and looked for a man to send over to check the Rangers' position. His eyes fell on Boots, Diehl's thug. Boots angered and scared Jenkins all at the same time. Boots ignored most of the things he said, but Jenkins knew he didn't want to get into a fight with the man. If he wanted to get rid of Boots, he would have to find an excuse to shoot him.

"You!" Jenkins pointed at Boots, then at the last place where they knew the Rangers had camped. "Get over there and find out where they are. The tin stars, I mean."

Boots stared at him insolently, taking his time deciding on whether he wanted to do it. Jenkins slid his right hand down toward the Colt in his gun belt. Boots continued to stare, letting his gaze slide down to Jenkins's gun belt and back. Finally, he turned, grabbed the reins to his horse, and began leading the horse toward the campsite at the base of the canyon wall. He didn't bother to glance back.

Jenkins watched him go, wondering if Boots would come back. For that matter, would Diehl come back? He decided it didn't matter in either case. He was better off without both of 'em, now that he had Diehl's money.

Another question nagged at Jenkins. Where were the settler's cows? Farther back into the canyon, obviously. Most likely on the other side of the wagons, keeping them penned against the east and north walls. That's what Jenkins would do with them, anyway. First, they had to solve the problem of the settlers and the Comanches. And the Texas Rangers, Jenkins growled to himself.

As the afternoon sun faded, Jenkins swung his field glasses from the settlers' camp to look to the north, where he could see someone riding in. After another few minutes, he knew he was looking at his scout, Carlos. Lowering the glasses, Jenkins watched until he could see Carlos without the glasses. He allowed himself a grim smile of satisfaction. He hoped the Comanches wouldn't be far behind Carlos with revenge on their minds.

He put the field glasses on Carlos again as he rode within two hundred yards of the settlers' wagons, then turned, moving toward the place where Jenkins had told him they would make camp. Jenkins lowered his glasses and turned, then heard a loud boom. He swung back around and lifted his field glasses to look at Carlos. Carlos was out of his saddle and down. The horse bolted for several yards, then stopped to graze. Carlos stayed down.

We stayed in our position above the settlers' camp all day, seeing almost no movement out there. By late afternoon, we saw a single rider coming toward the canyon wall below us, on a direct line for the settlers' camp.

McNelly watched him come for a few minutes, then

turned and talked to one of his men, who went to the supply wagon and rummaged around for a few minutes before coming back with an 1861 Sharps rifle. That wasn't what caught my attention. It had a sniper's scope on it.

I turned and looked at McNelly, who grinned briefly and pointed at the guy holding the Sharps. "He ain't used it for anything except deer up to now," McNelly explained, "but I hear he's a *can't-miss* shot with that Sharps. Good time for him to show me, I figger."

I turned and watched the lone rider still coming toward us. "You don't mind if it gives away our position?" I asked.

McNelly thought that one over, then shrugged. "It'll be one less of them to deal with when they come after us. The Comancheros will probly think it came from the settler camp," he concluded. "It might give the Comanches something to think about when they get here if they're following that guy. They'll know he's their enemy, or that's how I expect the Comancheros have set it up, anyway. The Comanches are following somebody that took a shot at them. If they think one of the settlers shot their enemy, maybe they'll pull off."

I backed off and watched while the Ranger laid down and balanced the Sharps across a log. He drew a bead on the lone rider, tracking him through that scope while the man drew closer, then turned and started riding toward the Comanchero camp. When the Sharps boomed, it came so suddenly I jumped. Turning to look down into the canyon, I saw the rider was down. I kept watching for a long time, but he never moved.

McNelly moved forward, nodded at his sharpshooter, and clapped him on the shoulder when the man stood.

He bent down again, laid a blanket over the Sharps, and
stowed it behind a log, ready if he needed it again.

————

Two hours passed, and we were mighty uneasy up there,
scanning the canyon floor. Three of us had field glasses,
including me, and we watched as the shadows stretched
out, sure the Comanches would come tonight. They
didn't disappoint me.

They came in at dusk, almost looking like ghosts
down there. I knew it was Black Hawk right in the
middle, riding a powerful bay. I guessed it was a stallion.
Hard to tell from up here, I thought. They came at a trot,
stretched out in a line, carrying rifles in one hand, all of
them that I could see, anyway. I did a silent count,
hearing McNelly as he eased up beside me.

"How many of 'em came?" he muttered.

"All of 'em," I said. "I make it to be twenty-four."

McNelly growled under his breath. We had hoped
they might leave a few back to protect their women and
children, but it hadn't happened.

They stopped to examine the dead man on the
ground, then gathered around Black Hawk. He sat and
stared toward the settlers' wagon. If they were going to
pull back, now was the time.

A random shot sounded from the wagons below, and
I lost all hope they would leave quietly. The Comanches
pulled off to their left, lining up side by side. The attack
was coming. They were angry enough or confident
enough to charge the wagons.

"Smart," I mumbled under my breath. "They'll come

in low and leaning over the horses' necks, not giving the settlers a straight-on shot." McNelly passed behind us.

"On my command," he said. "Not before." He turned to his sharpshooter, who was stretched out behind the log with his Sharps again. "Campbell?" he asked. "Have you got a shot?"

"Sure do," Campbell answered. "I can take out the chief."

"No!" McNelly blurted. "Not Black Hawk. If we can do enough damage, he will be the one smart enough to talk peace."

Campbell mumbled something and shifted his aim ever so slightly. I was watching through the field glasses when the Sharps boomed again. The brave to the left of the chief was slammed backward, arms flying up in the air. He tumbled off the back of his horse.

I swung to look at Black Hawk. He was stunned, I could see, but it didn't stop him. He leaned over his horse's neck, uttering a shrill war cry, and led the charge. The warriors closed in around him on both sides, guiding the horses with their knees and firing into the wagons.

They closed within a hundred yards and kept coming. I sighted in on a brave in the middle of the pack and waited.

"Now!" McNelly barked.

A dozen rifles sounded with a tremendous crash. I saw my guy slip slowly off the side of his horse, then bounce on the ground. His horse swerved into another Comanche, and I got off a second shot. The settlers joined in from below, and suddenly, there were a lot of horses with no riders down there.

Black Hawk barked a command, and they wheeled

and retreated. We had taken them by surprise from up here. I knew it wouldn't happen twice.

"How many did we get, do ya think?" It was McNelly again. I stared below, trying to see the retreating warriors. Even with the field glasses, it was getting too dark to be sure. I shrugged.

"Maybe seven or eight down for good," I answered. "I think they've got enough left to try again, but maybe not tonight. First light, that would be my guess." I stared through the glasses, trying to find them out there, but they had melted into the dusk. I didn't figure they had gone far.

I swung my glasses to the left, trying to find the Comanchero camp, but that was no good either. They had hidden it too well. We would have to take turns on watch and wait for the morning.

CHAPTER 10

DUELING SCOUTS

Dust was in the air off to the right, visible even in the fading light, and the mooing and thunderous sounds of a stampede were impossible to miss. I trained my field glasses on the dust, trying to see the cattle, but there was nothing else to see.

I set the field glasses down and looked over at McNelly. "They've taken the cows," I said.

McNelly nodded sourly and stared down into the canyon. As we watched, we heard a gunshot, then three more.

"Somebody probly got hisself shot guarding the cows," McNelly observed. I was afraid McNelly was exactly right. Hopefully, only one settler was down. There had been several gunshots.

"There's still nothing we can do until morning," I observed. "And maybe if those Comanches were short of food, they'll just take a couple beeves back to the main camp to feed everybody. That could make things simpler."

McNelly nodded thoughtfully. "Could be," he agreed. "Could be."

———

Diehl was up and moving at daylight, mostly because he'd had a terrible night of sleep. Mumbling to himself and in a foul mood, he moved steadily south and east, holding back from the edge of the canyon. He had no intention of being seen up here. Mostly, Diehl had started to wonder if it was a good idea to stick around this canyon at all.

Jenkins had Diehl's money. He wouldn't see that money again if he left, but the odds weren't looking as good for taking this herd as they had when he had left Ft. Worth. McCabe had apparently come out here with a group of Rangers, and Diehl had already made his try at shooting McCabe. That's why he was out here by himself, on the edge of the canyon right now. McCabe had to go home eventually. Maybe that was the place to wait for him.

By the time Diehl skirted the canyon edge as it turned around the eastern corner, he pulled up, dismounted, and tethered his horse to a mesquite tree. A short walk brought him to the edge of the canyon wall. Diehl dropped to one knee, shaded his eyes, and looked south toward the mouth of the canyon where he'd been yesterday.

The first thing Diehl saw was the cattle. That was the reason he'd come here in the first place. He had to admit, it was an impressive herd, and he couldn't see all of it. It's just that the Comanches wanted it, too, and the Rangers were trying to stop both parties from getting their hands on the herd.

Diehl rose and headed back to his horse. He decided to ride closer to the canyon entrance, but he didn't plan to rejoin the Comancheros today. For one thing, the Comanches were headed this way, and for another, he wasn't sure just how welcome he was back at the camp with Jenkins and Murphy. No, he would stay up here above the canyon wall for one more night. By morning, he might decide if it was time to cut his losses.

———

As luck would have it, Diehl knew it was time to cut his losses well before morning. After riding south for another hour, he dismounted and looked back down into the canyon, just in time to have a good view of the Comanches riding in and attacking the settlers. Only it didn't turn out the way Murphy, Jenkins, and the boys had it planned. Actually, Diehl knew now he was lucky he hadn't ridden right into McCabe and the Rangers, armed to the teeth and loaded for bear.

The Rangers had stationed themselves above the settlers, who had now drawn their wagons into a semi-circle, and with the fire pouring in from the canyon wall above them for support, they routed the Comanches. When the remaining warriors turned and stampeded the herd, everything was happening right below him.

One settler was trying to guard the herd, and the Comanches made quick work of him, shooting him down and stampeding the cows down the canyon. Diehl watched the herd disappearing in the distance. Now, his decision was simple. No way he would smack the back of a horse all over the canyon, rounding up cows and fighting off Comanches. He would wait for daylight and return to Ft. Worth for a few days.

To be exact, he would visit the White Elephant Saloon for a couple of days. He liked that place. He just wondered how he could find Boots and bring him along. The man was useful, especially in a place like Hell's Half Acre.

Little did Diehl know, but Boots was way ahead of him. He had sized up the situation when Jenkins had sent him to scout the Ranger camp. Finding them gone, there was nothing to keep him around that place. Boots was already well down the trail. He'd been thinking about Hell's Half Acre and the White Elephant Saloon all the way.

———

Black Hawk assigned two warriors to drive two cows back to the main camp to feed the women, children, and the old. He assembled the rest of the braves after they had stampeded the herd. Black Hawk knew this canyon better than anybody, except maybe a couple of his warriors. He had eleven men left after sending off the two, and he knew there was a way to get at those men who had fired from the top of the cliff. He wasn't ready to quit, but he had no intention of running into those guns again.

Black Hawk led his men to a steep, narrow trail winding up the walls of the canyon. They dismounted and led their horses up toward the top. It was a slow climb, and they still had a long way to go when they reached the top, but they could get to those hidden guns above the canyon. Each warrior would bring a rifle, and also a bow and arrows. It would start as a silent attack at dawn.

———

Pike Hardy had pushed the men hard to reach the canyon. Alternating mounts, they had made it in four days. He could only hope that was soon enough. He had a scout out in front of the men, an Arapahoe known only as Pye, who was the best scout at Fort Union. Maybe, Hardy thought, the best scout in the Army. As the sun set on the fifth day, he was at the head of the column, thinking about stopping and setting up camp, when he saw Pye returning from his scouting.

Pye, a man of few words, rode up and halted. He never seemed to bother with saluting, but Pike valued him too much for his tracking skills to worry about that. Pye pointed behind him. "Canyon there," he said simply. "Half mile. Good to camp here."

Hardy turned and gave the order. The men dismounted and began setting up camp. Pye drifted over and got some food to eat, squatting on his heels and shoveling the food in with one hand while he held a metal plate with the other.

Hardy waited for the man to finish. Pye set aside the empty plate and looked at Hardy, waiting.

"I need you to scout tonight. Can you do that? Need sleep?"

The Arapahoe shook his head and waited.

"There might be several groups up there," Hardy explained. "Settlers, Rangers...you know Texas Rangers?"

The scout nodded.

"Maybe Comanche, maybe Comancheros...bad men maybe dressed as Indians. You know?"

Pye nodded again.

"I need to know who's there and where they are," Hardy explained. "As much as you can tell me, be back before dawn."

The Arapahoe nodded again, grabbed his horse and rode off into the gathering twilight. Hardy turned to assign watch shifts, telling the men to get sleep when they weren't on watch. Tomorrow, he said, could be a long day.

———

Murphy was staring up at the cliffs above the settlers. His anger was settling down to something more like calculated revenge. Things hadn't gone the way he wanted. He had expected the settlers to be routed by now, with cows ready for the taking and the Rangers out there in the canyon, watching for Comanches.

As it was, the Comanches had been hit hard, the settlers were still in their circled wagons, nobody had gotten a shot off at the Rangers, and the cows were scattered from here to breakfast. Now what, he wondered.

To top things off, his scout had been killed, Diehl and his thug Boots were nowhere to be seen, and Jenkins, who had hired him and started this whole thing, was looking like he'd had all he could stomach and might be ready to pack it in.

Muttering to himself, Murphy kept staring at the cliffs. The key, he decided, lay in what the Comanches would do next. Or not do, he corrected himself. What would he do? And did that make any difference? No telling what an Injun was thinking, that was his experience.

What if, he wondered, they just took a couple of beeves and went back to the other side of the canyon? He didn't like the odds of fighting the settlers and Rangers without the Comanches getting in on it.

On the other hand, what if Black Hawk wasn't ready to quit? What if he could get up those canyon walls and attack the Ranger camp? A small smile grew on Murphy's face as he stared up at the canyon walls. If that happened, he thought, no reason his boys couldn't join the party and wipe out the Rangers. The Comanches and settlers would be easier to deal with then.

Murphy turned and went looking for Jenkins. He actually was working for Jenkins, although he suspected Diehl had paid the bills, and Diehl was nowhere to be seen. The Comanches might have killed him. Murphy found Jenkins squatted by the campfire, gnawing on a tough piece of beef, and pulled him aside.

"I want to move the boys up there," Murphy blurted. He pointed at the top of the canyon wall. "Up there, near where the Rangers were this morning. Hidden, like, up there near 'em."

Jenkins stared at Murphy like he'd lost his mind. "Why?" was all he said.

"Black Hawk has gotta know where that shooting came from today," Jenkins growled. "He won't charge into those guns again. He might take a couple cows and go home, or he might just climb up those cliff walls over there and attack the Rangers. I'd do it at dawn if'n I was him. We can be waiting up there."

Jenkins looked doubtful, but he was listening. "You wanna let the Comanches attack from one side, then we attack from the other? What if the Comanches come after us?"

Murphy stared at the ground for a minute. "We wait just a little," he said. "We let 'em kill off each other. The Rangers will be in the middle, they won't have a chance. Mebbe there'll be four or five warriors left. We take them down or let them skedaddle. Then we take the cows. If the settlers protest, we shoot 'em."

Jenkins still looked doubtful, but he finally nodded his head. "Worth a try," he said grudgingly. "When are you gonna move the camp?"

"One hour," Murphy said. "I'll tell the boys."

Jenkins watched Murphy walk away, then went to find his one remaining man, Charlie. He pulled Charlie away from the fire and spoke in a murmur.

"Murphy plans to move us up above the canyon and set up camp there. If the Comanches attack the Rangers in the morning, we mop 'em up, that's his plan." He left off talking and stared out into the night.

"We stay back, at the edge of things," Jenkins finished abruptly. "If it goes down like he wants, we have to share some cows with Murphy's boys. But if it goes bad somehow, like I think it might, we clear out of there during the commotion. Ain't nuthin' here worth getting our heads shot off. We light a shuck outta this place and get on down the road."

Charlie nodded silently and moved off to find his bedroll and horse. He wasn't one to ask questions.

————

Dinner wasn't much, unless you like cold beans and stale biscuits. That was my fault, I'll admit that right now. The problem was, a campfire can get you killed in enemy country, and I had to consider that we were in enemy country.

As I had told McNelly, we had given away our position this afternoon. It turned out great, we all knew that, but we had two sets of enemies out there—the Comanches and the Comancheros. The Comanches for sure must know that somebody had fired from up here, and I was betting that the Comancheros knew it, too. And we were still here, where we had done the shootin' earlier today.

The settlers were our only friends around here, and they had to stay put. The Army hadn't shown up yet. I had just finished explaining all of this to McNelly, and I wasn't telling him anything he didn't know. The part that had us worried the most was the idea that the Comanches might sneak up on us. They knew this ground, and they had the skills.

I threw the cold beans and biscuits over the edge of the canyon. I wasn't that hungry. Maybe the birds would like it. I watched McNelly pace back and forth. Then he called for Carter, the guy who had been scouting for us.

"I need you to look around for us," McNelly told him. "On foot. I need to know if the Comancheros stayed where they were yesterday. That's the first thing. If they've stayed put, that's probly about all you can find out tonight. Keep an eye out for the Comanches, but just check down at the mouth of the canyon, and come back and tell me if the Comancheros are still down there. Careful, though. Be real careful."

McNelly watched his scout leave, then came and sat down on a rock. "Where do you think they'll come from if they come after us?" he asked.

I ran my hand through my hair and thought that one over. Then I pointed to the north, away from the canyon mouth. "If the Comanches come," I said, "they'll find a way up that wall and come from over there."

I looked around in the other direction. "Not so sure about the Comancheros," I decided. "Maybe from the south, exact opposite side. Maybe from the east, trying to drive us up against the edge."

McNelly nodded slowly, then set six men in positions facing north, in case the Comanches came. He set up two facing east and two facing south. I waited, watching him.

"Where do you want me?" I asked.

"Float," he said. "Just float and do the best you can. Try to get some sleep," he said over his shoulder, then walked away.

———

Carter moved off into the night, getting little help from the moon, which was less than half-moon strength now. The days and nights of activity were wearing him down, but he knew the next day could be a fight to the finish for their company. They needed all the scouting help they could get.

Taking his time, pausing every minute or two to listen to the night sounds, Carter made his way to the canyon entrance and started down the trail to get to the canyon floor. Things seemed almost unnaturally quiet, but Carter told himself not to get spooked over nothing. It was the middle of the night, and he didn't expect to hear much out here. He just had to get to the edge of the Comanchero camp, avoiding sentries.

The incline under his feet lessened, and now he was

on the canyon floor. After pausing briefly, he moved to his left. He wanted to skirt around the canyon wall and approach the camp from the side. He was less likely to run into a sentry that way.

Carter used the occasional scrubby mesquite tree or hackberry tree to shield him as he moved, ducking down into the tall stands of the wild grasses when he couldn't find cover from the trees. After moving about a hundred yards, he heard people moving—not one, but several.

Looking around for cover, he spotted a juniper tree to his right and darted behind it, crouching down and listening. He didn't have to wait long. Men walked past him, only about twenty-five yards away, followed by more men leading the horses, muzzled and being led in pairs. The entire camp was moving!

Barely daring to breathe, Carter watched them move past, trying to remember how many of them were still here. McCabe had killed one, and they had shot the scout from long distance. One or more must have gone with the scout to try to rile the Comanches. That would leave how many, maybe nine or ten?

Carter couldn't be sure how many had passed him. The light wasn't that good, and some had maybe been behind the horses. He thought all of them were gone now. He could barely see the last of them climbing the path out of the canyon.

He waited another ten minutes before moving. Finally, he eased out from behind the juniper tree, stretched his muscles, and followed the group. He needed to know where they were setting up camp, then he could report back to McNelly.

Carter had taken only a few steps before a tremendous weight landed on his back and bore him down to the ground. He didn't dare cry out—that would only bring the rest of them. His head struck the ground with stunning force. He was dazed, but not out. He could feel a kerchief being stuffed roughly into his mouth, then another tied around his head to hold the first one in place.

Carter struggled weakly, but waves of dizziness passed over him. Somebody tied his hands behind his back now, and his captor was hauling him to his feet.

"Move!" the man hissed in his ear. That was followed by a shove in the back.

Still dizzy, Carter fell on his knees and collapsed to the ground. His captor cursed him in low tones, dragged him to his feet, and began marching him forward, up the path and out of the canyon.

CHAPTER 11

RAID AT DAWN

Nighttime was your friend, but it was also your enemy. Pye had thought of nighttime in that way for many years now. It hid his movements and shielded him from his enemy. But it did the same for his enemies. He was very aware on this night of the enemies who were out there and what would happen to him if they captured him. The Comanches would have no mercy. He had no hopes of anything better if the Comancheros caught him.

Pye tethered his horse in a stand of juniper trees near the mouth of the canyon and took several minutes listening to the night sounds. He had ridden up closer to the canyon entrance earlier, then turned his horse and moved away several hundred yards to hide the animal. Pye was uneasy. He caught an occasional bird call that didn't sound right to his experienced ears. The Comanches might be moving. After thirty minutes of simply listening, he slipped toward the canyon entrance. He had a Colt in his waistband, but his hand rested on a

knife in that same waistband. Silence was more important than anything.

Advancing only a few feet at a time, it took him
nearly an hour to begin his descent into the canyon. Even
so, he considered himself lucky when the whinny of a
horse gave away the presence of men climbing up this
path.

Pye was glad he had worn his moccasins. They made
no noise as he moved off the trail and flattened himself
in the wildflowers, several yards off the trail. He kept his
face down, watching the feet of the men and horses as
they moved past him. When the last of them passed him,
he raised his head only slightly and watched them move
away. When they were out of his sight, he still didn't
move, watching and waiting.

His patience was rewarded when he heard footsteps
and the whispers of one man cursing another, moving
toward him on the trail. Two men went past, one in a
buckskin jacket with a few feathers shoved in his hair.
Pye's lips curled up in a soundless laugh. There was no
chance this man was a Comanche. This was a
Comanchero—just as deadly, but probably less skilled.

Pye focused on the other man, who appeared to have
a gag in his mouth. His hands were tied behind his back
—that much he could see clearly. Pye decided in an
instant. A Comanchero had taken another man prisoner,
therefore the prisoner was someone he would help.

Moving silently again on his moccasins, Pye slipped
the Colt from his waistband and reversed it to hold it by
the barrel as he slipped up behind the Comanchero.
There was just a slight thud as the Colt connected with
the man's skull, and he slipped to the ground. The prisoner didn't have to be told to stay quiet. He said nothing

as Pye removed his gag and cut the rope binding his wrists.

Pye steered the man out of the canyon and out to where his horse was waiting. The man was too unsteady on his feet to walk, so Pye loaded the man up on his horse and led them to the Army camp.

Pike Hardy saw them coming. He moved up beside his sentry and murmured to the man to let them come in unchallenged. Pye helped the second man down, and the two came to stand in front of Pike together as Pye made his report. When Pye had finished, Pike Hardy turned to the second man, who said his name was Carter.

Hardy cast a practiced eye at the sky overhead. He estimated it was only two hours until dawn—no time to waste.

"You were scouting for the Rangers?" he asked. Hardy got a nod in reply. He steered the man over to a flat rock and motioned for Carter to sit down. "Tell me what you know," he said simply.

Carter accepted a cup of coffee from Hardy and heaved a sigh. "Cap'n McNelly, Sheriff McCabe and ten Rangers are up at the top of the canyon, right at the edge, overlookin' some settlers, got their wagons circled down below against the canyon wall," Carter said. Got some Comanches, mebbe a couple dozen, attacked the settlers yesterday an' we drove 'em off."

Carter gulped down a couple sips of the coffee and finished up his explanation. "There's a band of bad 'uns, Comancheros, I guess you'd say. They were down in the canyon, but I ran across 'em coming out and somebody jumped me, tied me up and such. Your man here," Carter stopped to point at Pye, "fetched a thump upside the head of the guy that took me prisoner. Brung me here."

Pike Hardy looked over at Pye, who shrugged and nodded. "I think maybe Comanches are coming," he said. "Something not right out there, maybe they come up the canyon wall to attack Rangers." He tried to explain it better, but came up empty and shrugged again. He decided he'd said enough.

Hardy looked from one man to the other, then wheeled to call his sergeant. "Harrison!" he shouted.

A man ran up and saluted. "Have the men ready to move at dawn," Hardy snapped. "Mounted and ready to charge at my command," he added.

"Sir!" Harrison executed a sharp salute and dashed away.

Hardy moved to gather up his bedroll. He checked his Colt as he walked away, then stopped when he remembered something Carter had said. He chuckled softly. "McCabe and McNelly," he murmured. "We've crossed paths again. I'll ride the river with those boys any day."

———

At first, I heard only a whisper of sound. My brain told me it was the sound of a moccasin running over the dry grass and rocks. I put my fingers to my mouth and whistled to alert the others, then dropped and rolled to the rocks on my left. My eyes registered a dark shape, moving through the early gray light. I triggered the Winchester one time, and he dropped.

There was a jagged streak of lightning and a sharp crack of thunder. I saw them in that moment of vivid, flickering light. There were maybe five or six of them, coming with tomahawks and knives. They had counted on a silent attack to take us out.

I heard a sharp hiss, and the man next to me fell, clutching at the arrow in his chest. The man next to him had gone down, his gun clattering on the rocks. A Comanche stood over him, tomahawk raised. I rushed up and shot the warrior point-blank. He went down, and the Ranger he'd knocked down stared at me, not moving.

"Get up!" I shouted. I snapped off a quick shot with my Colt at another Comanche and missed the shot, but the attack had been broken. A few of them were melting away into the dim light.

I counted the number of men down—two Comanches and two Rangers. That left four of the Rangers to fight off the next attack, and I was sure there would be a next attack. I reloaded and ordered the others to do the same.

Gunfire sounded on my right. I swung to see McNelly's men being overrun on our east side. He'd posted only two men there, and they were both on the ground. The Comancheros had swarmed past them. McNelly's two remaining men rushed in from the south side of the camp to reinforce them.

The lightning flickered again, and I could see McNelly, pistol gone, swinging his Winchester like a club. His shirt was ripped open, and there was a Comanchero behind him on one knee, lifting a pistol to take aim. I fired off a shot and dropped the Comanchero.

The lightning stopped. Gray light was filtering in, but it was hand-to-hand fighting now, and I couldn't tell friend from foe. I pulled my knife and rushed toward the spot where I'd last seen McNelly. "Hold your ground!" I shouted at the four who had helped me repel the Comanche attack from this side of the camp. If the Comanches regrouped and came at us again, I thought, we are all dead. McNelly's men were too green to hold off a two-pronged attack.

I felt a blow on my right shoulder and went down, the knife slipping away from me as I reached out to break my fall. Someone dove and knocked me on my back, then a tremendous weight fell on me, and a pair of hands was around my neck, slowly cutting off my air. I arched my back, trying to throw him, but he was too heavy, and I was growing weaker.

I could see his face above me now, bending down as he choked me with all his might. I summoned my last strength and grabbed him by the hair, yanking his head down and smashing his nose into my forehead. He gasped and pulled back for just a moment, then those hands closed around my neck again.

I heard a crashing noise, and he slumped to the ground. I looked up to see McNelly standing over me. The stock of his Winchester was shattered. I staggered to my feet and tried to make sense of the noise I had just heard.

A bugle. It wasn't until I heard the pounding hooves and shouts that I finally made sense of those noises. It was a calvary charge!

The Comancheros made a run for their horses. I could count five of them, but they had no chance of reaching the horses in time. I could see the cavalry now, charging in a line, guns ready. "Halt or we'll fire!" came the command.

Two stopped and raised their hands. The other three kept running. Four or five shots rang out from the mounted troops, and just like that, the attack was over. I looked back to my left and saw only two of the four men I'd left to guard that side. There was no sign of the

Comanches, but I knew there had been a second wave. No doubt, the remaining warriors had melted away as soon as they heard that bugle.

McNelly was taking stock of his men. Only four of the ten were left standing. Five were dead. Another had a shoulder wound, but he was getting treatment from another trooper and looked like he'd pull through.

I counted three dead Comanches and five dead Comancheros, counting the three brought down by the cavalry. I saw McNelly moving out to greet an officer who had swung down off his horse, and I followed.

McNelly stepped aside, and I stared at Pike Hardy, who had fought alongside McNelly and me in No Man's Land last year.

Hardy grinned. "Always pulling your fat out of the fire, huh, McCabe?"

I stared at him. "Well, Pike," I said. "I never thought you were a handsome man before, but maybe I was wrong."

Hardy turned around, fished in his saddlebag, and came out with a flask of whiskey. He handed it to me. "Here ya go, Jake," he said. "I think maybe you need this more than I do."

———————

Hardy's troops had some fresh venison, the settlers coughed up some eggs, and the smell of breakfast cooking was mighty pleasant after what we had just been through. Hardy ordered some of his men to bury the dead, and we moved down to set up a camp near the settlers.

Only one settler had died. The Comanches had killed

Oates, the self-appointed leader with the brash mouth, while he was trying to guard his cows. The remaining settlers had buried Oates this morning and agreed to divide up his herd evenly.

One settler approached as we finished breakfast, and I cocked an eye at him, thinking he looked familiar.

"Williams, Dan Williams," he said. "I'm the one who came and talked to you after Oates shot off his mouth. Back when you first came to see us," he reminded McNelly and me.

"Right," I said. "I remember."

McNelly pointed at a rock next to the one he was sitting on. "Take a seat," he offered.

Williams sat down and looked around at McNelly, then at me. Pike Hardy came up and joined us. I made the introductions.

"We taken a vote this mornin' and decided we want to stay," he announced. "Unless you think the Comanches are still after us. We ain't plannin' to get ourselves killed out here if we can help it." He paused and looked at us. "Do you think the Comanches are coming back? And how many of 'em are there?"

"Not many," I said. "I doubt if Black Hawk has more'n six or seven warriors left, assuming Black Hawk is still alive. There were only a few of 'em slipping away after the Army showed up."

McNelly pulled at his chin and stared off into the distance. "Yep," he said shortly. "He hasn't got many left, and if he's got women and children and old folks in another camp down yonder, he can't afford to lose any more braves."

"He might wanna smoke a peace pipe," he said, almost to himself. "If I could speak the lingo, mebbe I would ride out there and see if he wants to bury the hatchet."

"I can do that," Pike Hardy said. "Speak the lingo, I mean."

We all turned and stared at him.

———————

Jenkins held back while the Comancheros charged. Charlie stayed at his side, content to let the other guys take the bullets. The Rangers down there were pretty green, from what he'd seen, but he knew of Jake McCabe and wanted no part of an even fight with McCabe. He glanced sideways at Jenkins. The man fancied himself with a gun, but Charlie wondered if he was as good as he thought he was.

Both men stared through the underbrush where they were crouched, holding their horses and listening to the shots fired to the north. It sounded like things were shaking out the way Murphy had hoped—the Comanches had launched a dawn attack. In front of them, Murphy and the rest of the Comancheros attacked, meeting little resistance.

Charlie stood and turned to tether his horse. He figured the battle was almost over, and it was time to get in there and get his share of the cows. Jenkins looked over his shoulder and hissed.

"Stay down! Our boys might take out the Rangers, but we don't know how friendly the Comanches are gonna be, now do we?"

Charlie shrugged and went back down on his belly in the underbrush. Jenkins had a point. It wouldn't hurt to hold off for a few more minutes.

The bugle call caught them both off guard for a few seconds, but the sound of the drumming hooves told them all they needed to know. Both men had spent enough time in the Army to know a calvary charge when they heard one. By the time Pike Hardy's men had wiped out the Comancheros, Jenkins and Charlie were mounted and slipping away from the canyon, moving quietly through the hackberry trees and underbrush. By the time the cavalry and Texas Rangers were cooking breakfast, they had struck the trail back to Ft. Worth, moving at a steady pace.

———

Diehl felt relief when he reached Ft. Worth. He'd traveled the trail from Palo Duro Canyon by himself, and he wasn't used to going anywhere without having paid guns and muscle to look out for him. Not to mention, he didn't expect to have to shoot his food and do the cooking. He had lost three hundred fifty dollars on that little trip to the canyon, too. What was he going to do about that? He wasn't sure, but he'd had his fill of Comanches.

After sleeping with his gun next to him for nine nights, worrying about Comanches and outlaws, he reached Ft. Worth. The first thing he did was to find a place to get a shave and take a bath. The second thing was to find a hotel, where he slept for sixteen hours.

With some food in his belly, Diehl decided to pay a visit to Hell's Half Acre before he made any further plans. McCabe was still back there at Palo Duro Canyon, so far as he knew, but maybe Diehl could make a move on the land back at Fredericksburg with McCabe out of town. To do that, he needed guns and muscle. With that in mind, he headed for the White Elephant Saloon, pushing through the batwing doors in the early evening, squinting through the smoke as he worked his way through the crowd, feeling only a little more comfortable now than he had felt out there on the trail.

Leaning back against the bar and sipping at his first beer, Diehl glanced around the room, wondering if he could recruit some men here to back him if he made a move on McCabe back in Fredericksburg. Diehl's attention was drawn to a man playing poker at a table across the room. The man sat with his back to Diehl, but there was something familiar about him—the thick shoulders, bull neck and the battered black hat. Diehl took his second beer with him as he moved a little closer.

The man pushed his chips to the center of the table, took his money, stood and turned while he stuffed the money into his pockets. When he lifted his eyes and saw Diehl, a slow smile crossed his face.

"Figgered I'd see you here before long," Boots mumbled. "That was a losing hand, back there in the canyon." He stared at Diehl through the smoky room, wondering if Diehl had enough money left to make it worth Boots's while to keep working for him.

Diehl returned Boots's stare, feeling in turns angry that Boots had pulled out of the fight at the canyon without a word to Diehl, then feeling glad he'd run into Boots here at the saloon. He still needed some dirty work done, and Boots could do the dirty work with the best of 'em.

Diehl pointed the way back over to the bar. "Let's talk," he said. "I'm buying. Whatever you want."

CHAPTER 12

THE WHITE ELEPHANT

Jenkins had plenty of time to think on the ride back to Ft. Worth. Stealing the cows had sounded easy. Who knew they were facing a stacked deck? Texas Rangers and McCabe, that was bad enough. Add in Comanches and calvary...he shook his head. Bad luck.

One thing he had decided on was his ride away from the Palo Duro Canyon. The sweetest setup he'd had so far was as a sheriff. Back there in Kerrville, posing as Abe Richards, that was his kind of deal. He needed to get back to something like that.

He'd left the area in a hurry, and he couldn't go back to Kerrville. But he happened to know the sheriff over in Fredericksburg was out of town, and maybe hadn't survived that fight in the canyon. Only McCabe and the injured Texas Ranger, Stanton, really knew about his Abe Richards identity and his time in Kerrville. He was pretty sure Stanton was dead. Maybe McCabe wouldn't come back.

Jenkins checked into a hotel when he reached town. Charlie didn't have enough money for the hotel. Jenkins told him to bunk in at the livery stable and meet him at the White Elephant Saloon later. Jenkins needed to check for a telegram or two from Baker, the guy he'd left down in Fredericksburg. That might tell him what he needed to know about going back to his stomping grounds down there.

Jenkins treated himself to a steak at a restaurant and thought about Diehl. The guy hadn't been seen since Murphy had sent him to bait the Comanches back there in the canyon. No telling if Diehl was still around, either. He'd known something about McCabe, though. He had tried to shoot McCabe. What had that been about? Jenkins shook his head. This was all pretty complicated, and he liked things to be simple. He left some money on the table and pushed back. He would start by checking for a telegram at the White Elephant. One thing at a time.

Jenkins didn't bother checking around the livery stable to find Charlie. No doubt he had already reached the White Elephant at least an hour ago. Jenkins walked a few blocks and pushed into the bar. He'd been right about Charlie. His helper/gunhand had joined a poker game and appeared to be well into a pitcher of beer. Jenkins walked by and dropped a couple of coins on the table next to Charlie. Might as well keep the man happy. Jenkins might need him later.

He moved to the bar and found the guy he had paid to hold any telegrams. He was expecting some from his man Baker, who he'd left in Fredericksburg to keep an eye on things and report back. There was only one message. He frowned when he looked at it—the telegram was about three weeks old. Jenkins opened it and scanned what Baker had to say before cursing under his breath and stuffing the paper in his pocket.

The telegram from Baker was a plan to rob the bank in Fredericksburg. Either Baker had done it by now or he had gotten himself arrested trying. Or killed. Three weeks was a long time. Jenkins cursed under his breath again and ordered a whiskey. He was lifting his glass when a voice in his ear made him jump and spill the drink.

"You owe me three hundred and fifty dollars."

Jenkins half-spun to see Diehl standing, thumbs hooked into his belt. Jenkins choked off the answer he had in mind when he saw Diehl's thug, Boots, standing right behind him.

Jenkins gave both of them a long stare while he casually downed his shot of whiskey and reset the glass carefully on the bar.

"It was a business deal," Jenkins said casually. "We both lost money."

He waved for another whiskey and eyed Boots carefully from the corner of his eye. His mind raced, and he thought about what that cattle rustler Murphy had told him back there at Palo Duro Canyon. Diehl had been asking questions about Jake McCabe. There was some kind of connection there.

"I lost a lot more than you did. I think we need to even that out a little bit." As Diehl spoke, Jenkins was uncomfortably aware the Boots was moving around Diehl.

Jenkins picked up his second glass of whiskey and decided to gamble on Diehl's connection with McCabe.

"Too bad," Jenkins said, as casually as he could, considering how close Boots was getting to him. "I could help you get even with Jake McCabe." He drained the glass and set it on the bar, glancing sideways as he did so. He'd struck a nerve, that was obvious.

————

Two hours later, Jenkins had long since switched to beer. He needed to keep a level head. Diehl, suspicious at first, had told most of his story about the ranch and the land he'd owned near Fredericksburg, and how McCabe had gotten himself elected sheriff and chased Diehl out of town. Now, the ranch belonged to McCabe and his wife. And the wife's family. That's what it sounded like to Jenkins.

Charlie stood, left the poker table and joined Jenkins. Along with Boots, they were all staring at Diehl, waiting for anything else he wanted to tell them about the setup he'd had down in Fredericksburg until McCabe had taken it all away. According to Diehl, anyway.

"Had my own sheriff down there, I did," Diehl announced. The words were getting a little slurred. "Gutless, he was. Let McCabe run him right off."

Jenkins's ears picked up when Diehl started talking about the sheriff in Fredericksburg before McCabe. Being the sheriff over in Kerrville was the best deal he'd ever had. It was a lot better than chasing cows and Comanches around that canyon out there. If he shaved his beard, cut his hair short, got himself a new name and some new clothes, maybe Fredericksburg could be his next stop.

"Why didn't you just get yourself another sheriff who could run McCabe off?" Jenkins asked. "You said you ran that town. Why didn't you just do that? Get somebody to chase McCabe out?"

"Tried to," Diehl slurred.

Jenkins leaned forward. "What do you mean, you tried to?" he said.

The small part of Diehl's brain that was still working told him to stop talking. He had hired a gunfighter to handle McCabe, and McCabe had cut him down in the middle of Main Street. Diehl decided to keep that to himself. He shrugged.

"Didn't work out." Diehl pushed his whiskey glass away and stared across the table at Jenkins. "You gonna help me get that ranch back? What's it gonna cost?"

Jenkins leaned back and spun his beer glass around on the tabletop. "I was a sheriff once," he announced. "Best deal I ever had. Maybe you could help me be the sheriff in Fredericksburg after we get rid of McCabe. I'd like that."

Diehl stood, wobbling slightly, and extended his hand across the table. "Deal," he barked.

Jenkins nodded and shook the hand Diehl offered. Diehl pointed at Charlie. "You're gonna need somebody besides just him," Diehl said, holding on to the table with both hands.

"How many?" Jenkins asked. "Two more?"

Diehl considered that while he tried to keep the room from swimming around him. Boots reached out to steady him. "Yeah, I guess," he mumbled. "Two. If they're good." He turned to go, and Boots steered him out of the White Elephant Saloon.

On the way out the door, Diehl realized he knew almost nothing about Jenkins. He'd been a sheriff before, that's all Jenkins had revealed. Diehl shrugged and stumbled out to the sidewalk. He would find out more tomorrow. They needed to be headed for Fredericksburg by then. He didn't know if McCabe was dead or alive. But, if he was alive, Diehl needed to beat him back to town.

Jenkins finished his beer and stared around the room. He needed two gunhands. He ought to be able to find them before he left the saloon tonight.

———

We sat around a small campfire with the settlers. We had buried the dead. We had only five active Rangers, counting McNelly and me. Five were dead, and one man was recovering from an injury, unable to ride. Pike Hardy had lost nobody in yesterday's battle, so we had twelve soldiers with us. There were four men there at the campfire representing the settlers. With Oates gone, Dan Williams seemed to be their spokesman. He was an enormous improvement over Oates.

"What we want to know," Williams said, "is whether we can make some kind of peace with the Comanches and live here with our families. We don't want to be watching over our shoulders for Black Hawk all the time. And I don't expect the Rangers or the Army to stay here from now on, right?"

McNelly and Hardy nodded at the same time. Neither of them had orders to stay in the canyon after some kind of permanent situation could be worked out—whether that was a peace agreement, or the settlers moving out. Or the Comanches moving out. That last one seemed unlikely.

"It seems like a good time to talk peace with Black Hawk," I pointed out. "I don't think he's got over six or seven warriors, he's got women and children to think about, and it's a big canyon. He might just see the sense in sharing it."

"We need to see if he'll talk," McNelly agreed. He glanced over at Pike Hardy. "Can you send your scout out to take a look-see? He can take my scout with him if he wants to. We need an idea where Black Hawk and his braves are right now."

"Already sent Pye out to do some scouting. He'll do most of it after dark, but I expect him back by sunup with news on where the Comanches are. He likes to work alone, so he didn't take your scout with him."

"Another man might just get in his way," McNelly agreed. He looked around the circle. "Are we agreed we'll be ready to move out at sunup?" He looked at the settlers.

"We'll come." Williams jerked a thumb at his chest and pointed at one other man. "We'll ride with you."

"Okay," McNelly agreed. "We'll have our whole force out there, but we'll ride in plain sight, and when we get close, just McCabe, Hardy and I will ride out ahead and wait to see if Black Hawk wants to come an' talk things over with us." He looked at Hardy. "You're sure you can speak the lingo?"

"Yep. Dead certain," Hardy told him. He said nothing more, and McNelly didn't press him on it.

"Sunup, right here," McNelly said.

———

Pye rode into the settler's camp a little after sunup. I knew he had been up all day and all night, but he didn't look tired to me. Maybe, I thought, he's just good at puttin' a good face on things. I handed him a steaming cup of coffee and he looked at it like he'd just drawn four aces.

Hardy walked up, and his scout didn't waste any time. "Two days' ride," he said shortly. "Make camp tonight, see Black Hawk camp tomorrow." He pointed north and west. "Black Hawk move farther away. Woman and children camp on other side of Black Hawk."

Hardy turned and pointed at one of his men. "Hostler, saddle up a fresh horse for Pye," he ordered. "We ride right after Pye has somethin' to eat."

I stared after the soldier as he trotted off to move Pye's saddle to a fresh mount. Hostler, now that name sounded familiar. Then it hit me. The skinny kid with the big Adam's apple. The one that could make the cannon, Old Napoleon, sing like a canary. He'd fought with us last year in No Man's Land.

Hardy saw me watching Hostler and laughed. "Yep, that's him. The kid that touched off Old Napoleon for us. He's put on a couple pounds since then." Hardy chuckled. "First one to volunteer to come with me."

McNelly walked up, and Hardy filled him in. I mounted up and rode over to make sure Williams and the other settlers were ready to go. They were.

We mostly rode in silence, stopping to water the horses when a stream crossed our paths. Pye rode out in front of us, but we weren't really worried about a surprise attack. Black Hawk was lucky if he had enough braves to get through next winter.

As the sun began to set, McNelly called a halt, and we made a small campfire for supper, then doused it and set out watches for the night. Hardy moved over and leaned against a log we'd dragged up. He took a moment to listen to the night sounds. We had sentries set up on all sides, but I guess he'd developed that habit.

What he said next took me by surprise.

"Last year, when we were on that trip to No Man's Land, you told me a man could do well for himself in Texas these days. You said I could come down and pay you a visit in Fredericksburg."

I sat up and looked over in his directions. "I did say that," I agreed. "I stand by both those things." I paused a moment. "I moved down to Texas just a few years ago. So did my wife and her family. Never been sorry or wished I'd done anything different. There was nothin' for me back home in Kentucky. Now it's home for all of us in Fredericksburg."

Pike Hardy nodded, pulled his hat down lower and leaned his head back to look at the stars. "I'm mustering out just as soon as this mission is over. Once you and McNelly think things are settled down an' peaceful, I'm heading up to Fort Sill in The Nation. Hostler, too," he added.

That was the longest speech I'd heard him make, and I had to sort through it in my head for a minute. "Hostler too, huh?" I asked. In my mind, I was wondering if Hardy wanted to come down to Fredericksburg with me.

Hardy chuckled. "Yeah, Hostler too. Old Napoleon won't be the same without him."

"Do you want to come back to Fredericksburg with me?" I blurted out. "You could look around, see if there's anything you might want to do. You got anything in mind?"

"Well," he said slowly, "I got a little pay saved from the Army. I could run a few cows with a herd goin' to Kansas if I need to. Not sure I'd be much of a rancher, or want to be a rancher. Mebbe after a drive I could buy a store. Or I could do some sheriffin' somewhere. I'd know how to do that without too much trouble."

"You could," I agreed. "You probly wouldn't have to look too far to find yourself a sheriff job."

"Where?" he asked.

"Maybe in Fredericksburg," I answered after thinkin' on it for a while. "Julia's been wanting me to be at the ranch full time, she doesn't like the trips and me bein' away from home. Says she's tired of folks swinging punches at me. I been thinking about it for a while."

Hardy leaned forward and half-turned to me. "I'd like to come down there and look things over when I'm done," he agreed.

"Sure," I said. "I might need to stay a couple days around here with McNelly and tidy things up. You could join me after you muster out and ride down there with me. Hostler, too, if he wants to. We've got an extra room in the house and spots in the bunkhouse."

Pike Hardy and I shook hands on it, and I headed toward my bedroll. I realized Boone might be getting tired of bein' my deputy, what with him having a new wife and owning part of our ranch. I would talk to him when I got back. If he wanted to move on from being my deputy, I could offer it to Pike Hardy. I had a feeling it wouldn't take long before he could replace me as sheriff if I decided to move on. I could take him around, introduce him, and help him get elected.

———

It was getting on toward noon the next day, with the sun overhead and the sweat startin' to trickle down my neck when we saw them, mounted up in a line and riding toward us. I counted seven of 'em. The big man in the middle riding a powerful bay caught my attention right away.

McNelly raised a hand to halt the men and looked over at Hardy and me. "We need to have everybody else stop here. Then the three of us need to ride out to meet them."

Hardy nodded and gave the command to his troops. The three of us rode forward slowly. Both sides stopped when we were about thirty yards apart. I couldn't read any of the expressions on their faces.

"I guess that's Black Hawk in the middle?" I asked.

McNelly leaned over and spit in the dirt. "I expect so," he agreed.

It was silent for several seconds. There was a little breeze blowing through the valley, and I found myself watching Black Hawk's feathers moving with the wind.

McNelly broke the silence. "Tell him we come in peace," he told Hardy.

Hardy raised his right hand slowly and spoke something. I couldn't understand a word of it, but it looked like those guys over there did.

Black Hawk said a few words. McNelly and I both looked at Hardy.

"He wants to know who the chief is," Hardy explained.

"Tell him I am the captain of the Texas Rangers, and I have come here to make peace in this canyon," McNelly said.

Hardy translated, and Black Hawk immediately answered.

"He wants to know about the pony soldiers," Hardy

explained. He spoke a few words to Black Hawk. I guessed he was saying he was the chief of the pony soldiers, and we had all come to make peace.

Black Hawk asked something, and Hardy answered immediately.

"He wants to know if our words can be trusted," Hardy said. "I told him our words are true."

Black Hawk stared at us for several seconds, then wheeled the bay around, waving at us over his shoulder.

"What does this mean?" I asked.

"Well," McNelly said. "I expect we're gonna smoke a peace pipe with 'em. Either that or they're gonna scalp us. One of the two."

CHAPTER 13

BLACK HAWK'S DECISION

Ten minutes later Black Hawk and his warriors pulled into a niche in the canyon wall, where we saw a few teepees. Against the rock face, they had built a crude corral to hold their extra horses. Black Hawk slid down off his horse, motioned at us, and walked toward one of the teepees.

I moved up alongside Pike Hardy as we walked behind Black Hawk. "What do they put in those peace pipes, anyway?" I asked.

Hardy shrugged. "No tobacco around here. The Comanches usually use herbs, some bark, and maybe a couple other things. It won't smell great, but make sure you take a good puff. Don't want to offend them."

I was assumin' we were here for the peace pipe. I didn't want to think about that scalping thing McNelly had brought up.

We ducked under the flap and into what I assumed was Black Hawk's teepee. Somebody had built a small fire in the middle of it. Black Hawk squatted on the ground cross-legged and pointed at the ground, wanting us to do the same. He reached behind him, and to my relief, brought out a long pipe and started stuffing some things into one end of it.

The pipe looked like red clay they had probably held in a fire to harden it. One end was covered with drawings and bright colors. Black Hawk finished stuffing the end of the pipe, reached out to pull a small twig from the fire, and puffed until smoke rose from the pipe. He passed it to McNelly, who passed it to me, and I handed it off to Hardy.

Pike was right about it not smelling too good, but I made sure I took a good puff, then fought down the urge to cough. Black Hawk looked around nodded, then spoke to Hardy. After Black Hawk finished, Hardy turned to us.

"Black Hawk says the settlers can live in their end of the canyon and will not be bothered by the Comanche. The Comanche and their women and children will live at this end of the canyon. They do not want to see the white man beyond the spot where we are now."

"Tell him I agree," McNelly stated. "Me too," I said.

Hardy turned and relayed our message. Black Hawk listened, stood and nodded. The peace had been made.

———

McNelly met with the settlers when we returned from the Comanche camp. He relayed the news, and Dan Williams confirmed that peace had been made with Black Hawk and what we left of his band. The settlers gathered around and asked some questions, but they seemed to have hope for the first time since I'd arrived there. You could almost feel the relief.

After a while, Williams came back with two of the

settlers to ask how long we were going to stay in the canyon. It hadn't been discussed, so McNelly huddled with Pike Hardy and me.

"How long can you boys stick around?" McNelly asked bluntly.

Hardy looked at me, then told McNelly his hitch in the Army was up, and he planned to go with Hostler up to Ft. Sill and muster out right away. That was news to McNelly, and he fished around for what to say next.

Hardy kept talking. "I will appoint my sergeant in command of this troop," he said, "and I'll tell him to stay as long as you think they should. I'll telegraph my captain back at the fort. When you're done with them, they can go home."

Now McNelly looked at me.

I looked over at Hardy. "How long do you think it will take you to ride up to Ft. Sill, muster out, and get to Ft. Worth?" I asked.

Hardy squinted off into the distance and thought that one over. "Mebbe ten days," was his answer.

I figgered it would take me a week to ride over to Ft. Worth if I kept up a good pace. I looked back at McNelly. "Three days," I told him. "I've got to get back to Fredericksburg after that."

McNelly nodded and stood. "Let me know when you're ready to go," he told Hardy. He looked at both of us. "I can't tell you what a difference you made," he said. "I won't forget it. You need some help down the road, you come find me."

———

The next three days went quickly. We helped the settlers round up some of the cattle that had strayed during the fight. They had decided to divide up the cows that had belonged to Oates. I was helping Dan Williams drive the six new cows he'd just gotten to join the rest of his herd when I had an idea.

"D'you suppose you can spare one of those extra beeves?" I asked him.

Williams turned and pushed his hat back, mopping his forehead with a kerchief. "Yeah, I don't guess that would hurt me none," he allowed. "What do you have in mind?"

"Good will," I answered. "A whole lot of good will. Those Comanches might be a little short on food, seeing as how they lost more than half of their hunters in that battle a few days back."

I watched while he caught on to what I was suggesting. A grin spread slowly across his face. "Good will," he agreed. "Some of that might come in handy."

We recruited the Army scout Pye to help us locate that camp again, cut out one of Williams's herd, and drove it across the valley. We camped the first night, leaving the steer near water and good grass, then drove it for another half day.

Pye, riding point, raised his hand and pulled up. We rode up slowly to join him. There were three braves just sitting their horses and watching us. Two of them broke away and moved toward us. The third, I was pretty sure, was Black Hawk.

As the two drew closer, I pointed at the steer and then pointed at them. They nodded and began driving the steer away. Black Hawk raised his hand, and I raised mine in return. We turned and rode away, rejoining the others at nightfall the next day.

When it was time to leave the next morning, McNelly and Williams rode with me to the mouth of the canyon to see me off. I waved my hat and set out for Ft. Worth, already thinking about getting back to Julia.

———

Diehl muttered under his breath as the railroad car bounced over a rough stretch of track. He looked sideways at Boots, who was asleep, his neck stretched back at an impossible angle. The man had been sound asleep for the last three hours. Diehl stood up to stretch, got thrown up against the window when the train veered sharply to the right, and sat down again.

Not that he regretted making the trip by train. First he would go from Dallas to Courtney, Texas, then he would catch a spur to Austin, leaving a hard two-day ride to Fredericksburg. Jenkins and his crew would have to smack the back of a horse for a solid six days. That's once Jenkins was able to get started. He was still looking for gunhands he thought could do the job against McCabe.

Maybe, Diehl thought, the delay was partly his fault. Maybe he shouldn't have told Jenkins about the time McCabe had taken down a known gunfighter named Al Vincent. That had been a shock. But, Diehl told himself, it wasn't like McCabe was grease lightning and Vincent hadn't cleared leather. It's just that McCabe stood his ground and made his shot count a little better.

Diehl shifted his position, muttered to himself some more, and braced himself up against the window with his coat wadded up to cushion his head against the glass. In any case, it was going to be another week before Jenkins and his boys arrived. That gave him time to look around and see what the situation looked like now in Fredericksburg. Plus, Jenkins had told him to look up Jenkins's man Baker and find out what he had been doing.

Diehl glanced over at Boots again, who had started snoring, head still tilted back over the back of the seat. Boots would have to do the asking around. Too many people might still remember Diehl. He would show himself when the time was right.

He fell asleep despite his efforts to stay awake and plan things in Fredericksburg. He awoke only when Boots started shaking his shoulder. "We're in Courtney," Boots mumbled. "Got to change trains here."

Diehl growled and nodded, grabbed his travel bag and followed Boots off the train. He would let Boots worry about getting the horses shifted over to the other train. Diehl wanted to walk around and get the stiffness out of his joints.

Sleep was the last thing on his mind as the train covered the ground to Austin. They collected their horses, picked up some food and supplies at the general store, and struck the trail to Fredericksburg. Diehl pushed Boots to keep up the pace and keep the stops as short as possible. They grabbed a few hours of sleep that night and struck the trail again at sunup.

If the horses hadn't been wearing down, Diehl would have pushed into Fredericksburg after dark that night. Boots pointed out how much the horses needed rest, so Diehl grudgingly stopped. It was around noon the next day when they rode into Fredericksburg.

Feeling bold for some reason he couldn't explain, he rode down Main Street, though his hat was pulled low just in case he might be recognized. He'd grown a heavy beard since the last time he was here, too. He glanced curiously from side to side as they rode down the street. Not much had changed, as far as he could see.

Pushing his luck, Diehl told Boots to stop at the café. His stomach was rubbing against his backbone after the last two days on the trail. Hat still pulled low, he followed Boots to a table and sat with his back to the room. His luck held when a girl came over to take their order. He had never seen her before.

Lunch over, Diehl shoved a couple of coins at Boots to pay the bill, rose and waited outside, leaning against the wall with his hat pulled even lower. When Boots emerged, Diehl pointed down the street at the telegraph office.

"Over there," he instructed. "Go in and ask if somebody named Baker is around town. Jenkins says he has sent a telegram or two up to Fort Worth."

Boots shrugged and led the way over to the telegraph office. Diehl stayed outside, but the door was open. He tried to hear the conversation inside, but only a few mumbling sounds reached his ears.

When he heard Boots blurt "What?", Diehl came away from the wall and lifted his head. He looked up to see a woman who had stopped in the street. She was staring at him. Diehl felt a shock of recognition. He knew her, but he just couldn't quite place how or where they had crossed paths.

He put his head back down quickly. When he glanced up after a few seconds, she had moved on. Diehl stared after her...Hawkins. She was one of the Hawkins family who had stolen his ranch! McCabe's girl. What was her name?

Julia! It came to him suddenly. That was Ike Hawkins's daughter and McCabe's girl. For all he knew, they were married by now. Diehl cursed the bad luck and cursed himself for being careless.

Just then, Boots came out of the door, staring at Diehl.

"Bad news, boss," Boots said. "Baker got hisself killed trying to rob the bank. 'Bout three weeks ago. They buried him up there at Boot Hill, outside town."

Diehl said nothing. He swung on his horse and led the way out of town. This hadn't started out the way he wanted at all. He knew a cabin outside of town where he planned to hole up now. He had built it as a hideout when he was just getting started around here. Maybe tomorrow he would send Boots back into town to get a telegram off to Jenkins. Nothing about Baker getting killed, he just wanted to let Jenkins know where they could be found. He would have to word that telegram carefully. Telegram operators could be nosy, and they could have loose tongues.

Julia hurried down the street and ducked into the sheriff's office. Boone swung his feet down from the desk, in a good mood today because the doc had taken the sling off his arm yesterday.

"What kin I do fer ya?" Julia, he boomed.

Julia held up her hand while she stared out the window. After a moment, she relaxed and turned around to stare at Boone.

"I think I just saw Virgil Diehl," she said, trying not to sound breathless.

Boone stopped in his tracks. "Yer kiddin," he mumbled. He stepped past Julia, grabbing up his shotgun and stepping into the street. "Where?"

Julia pointed. "Rode out of town, moving pretty fast. With some really big guy I never saw before," she told him.

Boone stepped to his horse, shoved the shotgun into the scabbard and rode away without another word.

Julia watched him go, then walked down to the telegraph office. She had to get word to Jake if she could. The only thing she could do was to send a telegram to the hotel where he stayed when he was in Ft. Worth. He usually stayed at the Metropolitan Hotel when he was there. She had no idea where he was at the moment.

She stepped inside the telegraph office, where a young man of about twenty was still learning the ropes. He smiled eagerly at Julia.

"Yes, ma'am, what kin I do for you"

Julia smiled back. "I can wait if you need to send a telegram for the gentleman who was just in here," she said.

"No, ma'am," the boy said. "He didn't send no telegram. He just asked about the feller who got hisself kilt a few weeks ago."

Julia felt a sinking feeling in her stomach, but smiled and wrote out a telegram message for Jake. She had to be careful, as she didn't want to sound an alarm that would wind up warning Diehl. She gave the boy the name of the hotel Jake used in Ft. Worth. The boy looked down at the message:

Dear Jake,
Today I saw the man who went to California

a few years ago. Stop
You remember, we did a land deal
with him. Stop
There was a very large gentleman with him. Stop
See you soon.
Julia.

The boy scanned the note. "I'll have it out in no time, ma'am," he promised.

Julia stepped outside and stared down the street. Diehl wanted to know about the bank robber Boone had shot. Had they been working together?

———

Jenkins was in a foul mood. His partners over the years had said that happened a lot, but for three days now, he'd been looking for a couple gunhands who were salty enough to stand up to McCabe in a gunfight. Jenkins figured he could do it himself, but why take the chance? Diehl had given him a hundred bucks to find a couple guys. Jenkins had already spent twenty of that at the White Elephant, and still no gunhands.

He'd sent his man Charlie to check out the other saloons, with orders to bring back somebody who knew one end of his smokewagon from the other. Jenkins looked at the watch in his vest pocket. What was keeping Charlie?

The doors pushed open, and Charlie walked in with two guys Jenkins hadn't seen before. The first one caught his attention. Big guy, long coat, double-tied down guns. Looked like he hadn't seen a barber in at least six months. He reminded Jenkins of a wolf. The second guy only rated a couple seconds of Jenkins's attention. He was a smaller version of the other one.

Jenkins's eyes went back to the *wolf*. Charlie walked over, and Jenkins shoved a couple chairs out, inviting them to sit.

The big one spoke first. "Heard you're lookin' for hands," he said. His eyes locked on Jenkins for a second, then he looked around the room.

"Maybe," Jenkins said cautiously. "What's your name?"

"Bryce," came the answer. The man waved at a server. "What's it pay?"

"Thirty," Jenkins answered abruptly. "Shouldn't take no more than two weeks, down to Fredericksburg."

"Heard you're goin' against Jake McCabe," came the short answer. "McCabe kilt Al Vincent, a couple years back. That'll cost ya fifty. And thirty for Shorty, here." He jerked a thumb at this partner.

Jenkins started to ask how the man knew about McCabe, but he decided not to. "Bryce," he said instead. "That your first name or your last?"

"Same thing." The man's whiskey arrived, and he tossed it down. His partner Shorty did the same.

Jenkins stared at the man for a while, then glanced at the partner again. He wanted to know more about this man, but he had a feeling he'd been told everything the man wanted to say. Jenkins had been in town here long enough. Time to get moving.

"Done," Jenkins said. "I got a few supplies to pick up in the morning. Meet you here at noon. We leave then."

"Half now," Bryce growled. He locked eyes with Jenkins when he started to object.

Jenkins opened his mouth, then closed it without

saying anything. He fished in his pocket and put forty dollars on the table. Then he turned on his heel and walked out, wondering at what point he had lost control of the situation. Charlie followed on his heels. When Jenkins reached the door and looked back, Bryce was waving for more whiskey.

CHAPTER 14

A SHOT IN THE DARK

I was standing in front of the Metropolitan Hotel, corner of Third Street and Commerce in Fort Worth. It was a pretty nice place—I think Julia was jealous she'd never been able to come and stay there with me just yet. It was on account of her that I was frustrated at not seeing Pike Hardy and Hostler. I'd been here only a day, but I had hoped they would be here when I rode in from the canyon.

I turned and walked toward a café for some breakfast, wondering what I would do with myself until Pike Hardy showed up. I hoped that would be today. When I don't know what else to do, I eat, so I had myself some steak, three eggs, toast and coffee. When that was done, I left thirty cents on the table and walked out to the street, wondering again what to do with myself. It was too early to go back and see if Pike Hardy had showed up at the hotel.

The livery stable was just another two blocks down the street, so I went and got my horse, Sherman, saddled up and rode over to the stockyards. I strolled around for a while, impressed at how many cows they had in those pens, being bought, sold, and staged for drives to Kansas. Folks said the railroad would come in a couple more years, and that might be the end of the drives to Kansas. I was a little sad about that—I knew some young cowboys who had made themselves a little money that way.

I put Sherman back in the livery and strolled around town for a little. They were proud of a new park they'd just opened. Being a country boy from way back in the hills of Kentucky, I thought it was pretty funny they had to set aside a little land just to have some trees and grass and bushes and such. It made me want to get back to my ranch.

Finally, when the shadows told me it was getting to be late afternoon, I headed back to the Metropolitan Hotel and walked into the lobby. Pike Hardy and Hostler had just checked in with the clerk. I walked over and slapped Hardy on the back.

"Dinner's on me," I promised them. "Just slap a little of that trail dust off and meet me back down here."

"Half hour," Hardy promised. "Dinner's going to cost you. Hostler and me have been livin' on jerky and beans for seven days."

I checked for messages, hoping for a telegram from Julia, but I had nothing. I sat down and fidgeted around in the lobby, just waiting.

We settled down in a diner a short while later, and I let them order what they wanted. Hostler ordered just about everything on the menu. Now I knew how he had gained weight since the last time I saw him.

Hardy leaned back and pushed the empty plate away after about a half hour. Hostler wasn't done yet, but I didn't want to interrupt him. That boy was concentrating.

"We've got a little pay from when we mustered out to keep us both going for a while," Hardy said. "Maybe we can look around for some work while we're planning what we want to do. You got any ideas of things we can look at?"

I pushed my beer glass around the table for a minute. "I got me a deputy who's somewhere between sixty and eighty," I told him. "I suspect he's closer to sixty, but he moans like he's eighty. Anyway, he might be tired of bein' my assistant. Just got himself a new wife, too."

I glanced over at Hardy. He looked interested.

"I could see if he wants to hang up the badge," I told Hardy. "I suspect he hasn't quit 'cause he wants to keep my back covered. If he wants to move on, would you want to be my deputy?"

Hardy nodded immediately. "I'd like that," was all he said.

I looked over at Hostler. "You could maybe help us out sheriffin', time to time," I said. "And there might be some work at the ranch, too. I could check with my father-in-law. I know you can ride."

Hostler nodded his head up and down several times, then went back to stabbing at what was left on his plate.

"Done," I said. "I'd like to leave at daylight, get back to town."

"You got trouble down there?" Hardy asked. "McNelly told me somebody took a shot at you, you in partikler back in the canyon, before the fight really started. You got some enemies might want to stretch your hide?"

I shrugged. "My biggest enemy is out in California, from what I hear," I said. "Haven't seen hide nor hair or him in a couple years. There's a few others I've arrested, might be out and drifting around. Anyway, I don't want to leave old Boone holding down the fort for too long."

Hardy nodded, and we all stood. "Daylight's okay for us," he said. "How long is the ride?"

"Six days," I said. "We ride steady for six days, we'll be there."

We left at daylight. Later, I found out I missed a telegram from Julia by just a few hours. It's one time I wish I hadn't been so prompt, leaving at the crack of dawn.

———

Slade Jenkins didn't like long trips on horseback, but he had to admit it gave him a chance to do a lot of thinking. Three days into the trip to Central Texas with his hand Charlie and the new guys, Bryce and Shorty, had given him a chance to do some thinking.

The attempt to rob cattle in the Palo Duro Canyon had been a disaster, he couldn't deny that. Who would've thought that not only would the Texas Rangers show up, but that the Army would come rolling in with a cavalry charge on top of it? A perfectly timed cavalry charge, no less.

Now, though, things seemed to be going his way again. He had a chance to set himself up as a sheriff, just down the road from where he'd done it the first time. He could organize a gang to rob travelers on the roads and take money from citizens, and he wouldn't have to worry about jail, since he was the sheriff. He would have to make an effort to disguise his appearance for a while, but very few people from Kerrville showed up in Fredericksburg, so he likely wouldn't be recognized.

Diehl had a history with McCabe, so he would both be hating McCabe and scared of McCabe. Jenkins could put that situation to work. There was money to be made off of Diehl, he was sure.

Jenkins put his mind to work, figuring out how he could go about replacing the sheriff until there was an election. He could rig the election, he was sure. It was just a question as to how he could get the town to support him in the meantime.

Scaring folks, threatening them. That worked the best. Maybe he could bribe a couple of others if he needed to. Jenkins looked around at the men riding behind him. Maybe Bryce could scare a few people, but it wouldn't work to shoot town officials and business owners. He had to scare them.

Boots! Diehl's thug. That's who could scare people. The fear of Boots coming around and stomping on them could make a few people support Jenkins.

The more he thought about it, the more Jenkins liked the idea. He could offer to let Diehl make use of Bryce and Shorty while he borrowed Boots. A small smile played across his lips. That's what he would do. He would borrow Boots and let him bully people in the town.

———————

Diehl nestled down into the underbrush behind a stand of burr oak trees, using his field glasses to watch the big stone house that had once been his. In the two hours he'd been here, he had seen the mother and two boys coming and going from the house. He knew the father, Ike, had a wooden leg, and he knew about the daughter Julia. He hadn't yet seen either of them.

Boots had been scouting the town for him, and Diehl expected to see Ike return to the house in another hour or two. Boots said Ike had been at the sheriff's office most days. Probably, Diehl figured, he was helping cover for McCabe while he was up at the canyon.

The one Diehl most wanted to keep track of was the old deputy, Boone. If Boone were out of the way, Diehl could move to install his own sheriff again, just like the old days. Jenkins would do for now if he didn't get too greedy.

The warm afternoon sun had its effect on him after a while, and Diehl drifted off to sleep. The sound of hoof-beats and a creaky wheel woke him up a short time later. Diehl grabbed his field glasses and trained them on the stone house. Both Ike Hawkins and his daughter were in a buggy, rolling up to the front door. While Diehl watched, they both went into the house. An hour later, nobody had come out.

Diehl wormed his way back from the underbrush where he'd been lying and crept to where he had tethered his horse, back in the woods. He mounted and rode away slowly, keeping the trees between himself and the house.

No sign of the old deputy. That was the one thing that bothered him. If Diehl could quietly take the deputy out of the picture, Jenkins might have a clear field to install himself as a temporary sheriff. Maybe, Diehl mused, he could have a couple of Jenkins's gunhands stage a robbery or two, getting folks worried about the safety of the town.

By the time Diehl reached the old shack he was using as a hideout, he had remembered the little house McCabe had set up on the property next to Diehl's old ranch. McCabe had bought that land and built the house on a bluff overlooking one of Diehl's pastures. That, he thought, was the place to check next. Maybe he could find Boone up there.

He waited in the shack for Boots to show up, cursing at the walls every time he heard a rustle out there. He had expected Boone to stay with him, but the man wanted to stay in a rooming house in Fredericksburg. Diehl suspected most of his pay was going to the saloon on Main Street.

Diehl's lips curled up in a sneer. Gambling had been good to him in California. He had plenty of money to keep paying Boots, he would just never let Boots know about that. He liked to keep people guessing about what he had or didn't have.

Finally, Diehl heard the creak of saddle leather and stepped outside to see Boots dismounting.

"Well?" Diehl demanded. "You been keeping an eye on the sheriff's office like I told you to do?"

Boots stared at him, blinked a few times, and leaned over to spit. "Yeah," came the slow and disinterested answer.

Diehl folded his arms over his chest. "And?"

Boots leaned over to spit one more time and wiped the back of his hand slowly across his mouth. "The old man with the wooden leg sits outside the office most of the time. Has his shotgun with him. Might be pretty handy with it. Mostly jest talks to folks or naps in the chair. Goes home around dinnertime."

Diehl waved his hands impatiently. "And the other one? Boone?"

"That 'un makes the rounds in town, rides out somewhere now an' then. Carries his Winchester like he was born with it. Wears a pistol, but I expect the Winchester is what he uses first. Might be pretty salty, that 'un. Might have to catch him by surprise afore he can get that Winchester up."

"That's what I'm gonna do," Diehl said smugly.

Boots stared at him. "You gonna bushwhack him?" His expression was hard to read. Diehl didn't really care about giving a man a fair chance, but maybe, he thought, maybe Boots did.

"I'm just gonna deal with him, that's all," he answered vaguely. "You get here before sunup tomorrow. I might know where to find him."

Boots didn't answer, he just gave Diehl a long look that might mean anything. Finally, he nodded, mounted up, and rode away into the gathering darkness.

———

Julia finished packing up the basket she had prepared for Boone and his new wife, Alice. Alice was mainly a city girl, and it was taking her a while to get used to living on the ranch. Julia paid a visit once in a while and brought some goodies with her when she did. Boone had taken Jake's old cabin overlooking one of the pastures. Jake had moved into the stone house on the ranch since the wedding, living with Julia and rest of her family. There was plenty of room, and Julia preferred it to Jake's cabin.

Picking up the basket, she left the ranch house quietly. The sun was just now peeking over the horizon, and she didn't want to wake anybody in the house. She stopped next to the front door and picked up her Winchester. Since the day she had seen Diehl at the tele-graph office, she carried it with her everywhere.

Julia moved along the edge of the pasture, near the

tree line. She had just enough daylight to find her way. It didn't hurt that she had traveled this path so often before the wedding when she came this way to see Jake.

Ten minutes' brisk walk brought her to an embankment leading up to the cabin. Julia moved past the well Jake had put in, then scrambled a little as she climbed, choosing carefully where she stepped while holding the basket in one hand and the rifle in the other.

As she reached the top of the embankment, Julia jumped suddenly and dropped the basket when she heard a gunshot. It came from directly in front of her. She heard a sharp grunt from Boone, who sounded like he was standing on the porch. She heard footsteps and another gunshot, followed by a shriek from inside the cabin.

Julia dropped to the ground with her Winchester in front of her. She swung her gaze from side to side, staring past the clearing in front of the cabin. As she watched, someone rose and lifted a rifle, sighting down the barrel toward the cabin.

Julia snapped off a quick shot. There was a loud oath from across the clearing, and she saw the rifle fall to the ground. She heard scrambling from the underbrush across the way. She held her ground right where she was, watching intently and listening for any sounds from the attacker.

———————

Boone stepped outside the cabin in the gray morning light, carrying a pan of water he'd used to wash up this morning. Alice insisted he pour the water on the flowers she had planted at the side of the cabin. Boone grinned even as he continued to mumble about watering the flowers. Used to be, he reminded himself, he could just open the door, throw the water out on the ground, and be done with it.

His years of living in the wilds and tracking game came in handy when he heard a slight rustle in the underbrush across the clearing. Boone froze where he stood, searching the bushes across the way. It could be a deer or a varmint, he reminded himself. Still, he wasn't a trusting man, and that had served him well on several occasions.

When he heard another rustle and saw movement, Boone sprang into action, taking two running steps, then diving toward the open door. At the same time, he yelled at Alice to get down and take cover inside.

Boone felt a punch in his upper right leg and fell to the ground near the door. He rolled over and crawled through the door into the cabin. Another shot sounded, and there was a splintering crash when the second bullet struck the edge of the door, sending splinters flying into the cabin.

Alice cried out and grabbed her arm when splinters struck her. Boone rolled again and kicked the cabin door shut with his good leg. He pushed himself to lie in front of the door, blocking it. For a moment, he could hear only his own heavy breathing. Then another shot sounded. It came from the side of the cabin and behind it. Boone heard a yell and a curse from across the clearing, then all fell silent.

Virgil Diehl wasn't a patient man, and even he would admit that. Most times, he saw no reason to wait for anything. If there was something he wanted, he just took it. That had worked out for him most of the time.

This morning, he had arrived at McCabe's old cabin before dawn and staked out a spot across the clearing where he had a good line of fire on the cabin door. Boots had said nothing when Diehl told him he only wanted to watch the cabin, but he had looked carefully at the rifle lying beside Boone. Boots was a brutal man, but he prided himself on giving everybody a fighting chance.

Diehl ignored the hired help and kept his eye on the cabin door. He chafed at the long wait, glancing overhead from time to time, mentally urging the sunrise to hurry up. Finally, he thought he heard some movement inside the cabin. In another ten minutes, he was sure someone was in there.

When the door opened, Diehl reached down and dragged his rifle to him, then lined it up on the cabin while the man poured out some water at the side of the cabin. There was enough light to tell him this man was Boone, the old deputy.

Diehl sighted down the barrel and slowly tightened his finger on the trigger. Suddenly, the old man bolted toward the door and dove. Diehl moved the rifle and snapped off a quick shot. Boone went down but crawled through the door, then moved to kick it shut.

Diehl rose just slightly to line up a shot at Boone as he lay on the floor, but then another rifle sounded, and he felt a burning slash across his ribs. He cursed and dropped the rifle. Boots dove and knocked him down, producing more swearing from Diehl. Boots slapped his hand across Diehl's mouth to silence him.

"Quiet, you fool!" Boots rumbled. "You'll get us both shot!"

After a minute or two of silence, Boots let go of Diehl and began crawling through the brush toward their horses. Diehl followed, still shocked and angry. Part of him was angry about being shot, the rest of his anger was at Boots for calling him a fool.

They mounted and rode away. Diehl could feel the blood seeping down his side where the bullet had grazed him. His anger cooled as he realized he'd been very lucky.

CHAPTER 15

BEFORE THE STORM

Julia waited for several minutes, torn between rushing into the cabin to help Boone and Alice, on the one hand, and not wanting to draw fire by moving, on the other. She had heard them rustling in the underbrush over there. She might have hit somebody, or maybe they were just badly startled when she fired.

Julie held her position on the edge of the bluff, straining to see in the gathering light and listening intently. Boone and Alice had gone quiet inside the cabin. She wasn't sure if that was good or bad. Finally, she heard horses' hooves moving away from her. She risked a peek over the edge and saw nobody.

Holding low with the gun out in front of her, Julia moved as quietly as she could to the edge of the cabin.

"Boone!" she called out in low tones. "It's Julia. I'm coming in!"

She waited for an answer. Jake had told her too many stories from the war about soldiers getting shot by their own sentries. Finally, she heard Boone's rasping answer.

"Come in. Got ya covered," he said.

Julia dashed inside and found Alice wrapping Boone's leg. She had cloth wrapped around her own right arm. Julia knelt and looked on while Alice finished the wrapping. Boone, she thought, looked pale, but he seemed alert.

"How bad is it?" she asked.

"Went clean through," he answered, stopping and gritting his teeth while Alice finished wrapping it. "Didn't break the leg, just knocked it out from under me when I went for the door."

Boone stopped and braced himself up against the edge of the bed. "Somebody bushwhacked me, for sure," he said. "I didn't hear nuthin' until that rifle shot knocked me down." He looked up at Julia. "I'm wondering if it's that skunk Diehl. You thought you seen him the other day."

Julie looked at him only briefly before nodding. "Same thing I thought," she said, "just as soon as the shooting started." She looked out the door. "They rode away," she said. "At least two horses. I'm going out there to take a look."

"Careful," Boone warned. He looked at his wife. "Shut the door behind her," he told Alice.

Julie skirted the edge of the clearing and moved to the area she had targeted with rifle fire just a few minutes before. She crept through the underbrush, finding an area where probably two people had been laying down. She could see the broken branches and crushed leaves. She followed a few faint footprints and saw a little blood on the leaves where at least two men had passed.

She found hoof prints a little farther on. There were

several tracks where two horses had been tethered, then tracks leading out to the trail that led to town.

Julia returned to the cabin, tapped lightly on the door and announced herself. Alice opened the door for her.

"Two men," Julia announced without preamble. "They rode off. One of them is bleeding, so I at least winged somebody."

"Good for you," Boone growled. He looked around. "We can't stay here and wait for those varmints to come back. We gotta get out. Now."

"Right." Julia turned and started for the door. "I'll get the buggy and take you down to the stone house."

"No!" Boone spoke so suddenly that it caused Julia to stop and turn in the doorway.

"The buggy's too rough a ride?" she asked. "I don't know how to get you down there..."

"Not a problem with the buggy," Boone rasped, puffing with the effort of talking. "I ain't goin' to the stone house. I'll just be a target for 'em down there and I'm not drawing yer family into the line of fire."

Boone paused and leaned back against the bed.

"Where, then?" Julia demanded.

Boone looked at both of them. "I started building me a line cabin out at the far end of the west pasture," he said. "Didn't get it finished, but I got the sides up and I slung a tarp over the top. Take me there. Take Alice back to the stone house with you."

"No!" Alice blurted. "I'll come with you."

Julia looked from one to the other and waved her hand in the air. "I'll get the buggy," she announced. "You two can settle this while I'm gone."

When Julia reached the stone house, there was no one home, for which she was grateful. As for Ike, she expected him to be at the sheriff's office. Her mother and brothers were out by the barn. She loaded blankets, food, and bandages in the wagon. She picked up two buckets for water and added those to the load, then hitched up her horse and drove the buggy back to Boone's cabin.

When Julia came through the door, she could tell that Alice had won the argument. She stood by the door, arms folded, jaw set in a firm line. Boone was still propped against the bed, looking down and shaking his head.

"Good," Julia said, "I can see I'll be taking you both to the line cabin. Boone, let's get you loaded."

It took both of them to lift Boone and help him to the buggy. They loaded him between the two of them, with Alice propping him up for the ride. Julia climbed in and followed Boone's directions to his line cabin. She didn't try to cover tracks or stay out of sight. She knew she had to get him there in a hurry to bathe and bandage the wound. Boone just gritted his teeth and hung on.

The trip to the cabin took longer than she'd hoped. They had to slow down frequently to make the ride a little smoother for Boone. As it was, Julia could see the sweat rolling down his forehead and cheeks by the time they arrived.

Julia and Alice helped Boone down, then each took an arm to get him inside. Julia took a quick glance around and was relieved to see an old mattress lying on the floor. They eased Boone onto the mattress, then brought in the supplies Julia had loaded, in addition to Boone's Winchester and Colt, which she left on the floor beside him.

"I'll bring more ammunition on the next trip," she promised Boone.

Carrying a bucket to the nearby stream, Julia brought

water back to a circle of rocks outside the cabin, which Boone had clearly set up for a fire. She went into the cabin and found matches. There was wood, she had noticed, behind the cabin.

After heating the water, she carried the bucket inside and washed the wound. Boone was surprisingly quiet. Julia looked up to see he had stuffed a rag in his mouth. When she had finished, Julia wrapped a clean rag around the wound. Boone collapsed back onto the mattress with a sigh and fell asleep within a few minutes.

Julia motioned for Alice to follow her outside. "I have to go now," she told Alice. "The best thing you can do is keep the wound clean and let him get as much sleep as he can. Food when he's hungry, of course."

She stopped and looked up at the sky. "I think we might get a little rain later, which will help to cover our tracks. I'll get the doctor to come out here and look at him if I think I can do it without being followed. I'll bring more food and some ammunition in the morning."

Alice nodded grimly, then stepped forward to give Julia a hug. "Thank you so much," she said, tears welling in her eyes. "I know he's ornery a lot of the time, but..."

Julia laughed. "We wouldn't have Boone any other way," she assured Alice. "He's family to us." She mounted and rode away, already starting to worry if the same men would attack the stone house. She wondered if Jake had gotten her telegram.

———

Boots took another swig from his flask and peered down the road for about the twentieth time since he had taken up his post. Diehl had sent him out here about two hours ago to keep an eye out for Slade Jenkins and his crew of gunslingers. Boots growled under his breath. If Diehl wasn't such a coward, he would take care of things himself.

Boots took another swig from the flask and reminded himself that Diehl had money. That's the only reason Boots had stayed with him. He planned to separate Diehl from a little more money before he left.

Another glance down the road showed some dust rising in the distance. Boots stowed the flask and hunched down behind the trees, waiting for the travelers to reveal themselves. As they drew closer, he estimated there were three or four riders, which sounded about like what he and Diehl were expecting.

When they were about fifty yards away, Boots could recognize Jenkins riding out front. Boots stepped onto the road, and it was almost the last thing he did. At least two of the riders threw down on him. Jenkins threw his hands in the air when he recognized Boots.

"Hold it!" he yelled. "It's a friend."

Boots heaved a long sigh and promised himself he would go a little easier on the flask for a while. These guys had trigger fingers.

He stepped slowly toward the riders, careful to keep his hands in the air and in sight. "Diehl sent me," he told Jenkins, warily eyeing the riders behind Jenkins. He knew one of them from the canyon, the other two were strangers.

"He wants me to show you the way to his hideout," Boots informed Jenkins. He pointed toward the trees. "I got my horse over there. It'll take about a half hour."

"Lead on," said Jenkins.

Boots led the way for about thirty minutes, as

promised, leaving the road to follow a faint trail threading its way back into the woods. He pulled up abruptly in front of a three-sided shack with a collapsing roof. Rocks from a collapsed chimney lay all around the shack.

Jenkins reined in his horse and stared at the building. "What do you call this?" he asked Boots.

Boots shrugged. "Diehl calls it his shack," he replied. "I call it a pile of boards waitin' to fall down. I won't sleep here." He dismounted and tethered his horse.

Jenkins nodded slowly, dismounted, and motioned to his men to do the same. The door to the shack creaked open, and Diehl shuffled out, holding his ribs.

"Come in," he said, waving at Jenkins.

Jenkins stared at the shack. His gaze traveled from the walls to the roof, then down to Diehl. He shook his head slowly from side to side.

"I don't think so," he answered. "We'll just talk outside."

Diehl shrugged. "Suit yourself." He seated himself on a rock and waited for the others to join him.

"I found the old deputy, Boone," Diehl blurted. "Got some lead into him, mebbe killed him. He's out of action, for sure."

Jenkins said nothing. His eyes traveled from Diehl's face, down to his ribs, then back up. "You're sittin' a little stiff," he observed. "Mebbe the old man got a little lead into you."

Diehl forced himself to sit up straight. He fought down the groan that came to his lips, but couldn't cover the wince of pain that shot across his face. "He creased me, that's all. Lucky shot." Diehl was pretty sure somebody else shot him, maybe from behind the cabin. He didn't want to get into that. It could've been the girl.

"Don't matter, nohow," Diehl continued. "I'm gonna go back there and finish off the old coot."

"What if he's gone?" Jenkins asked. "You think he's just gonna sit there for you to have target practice?"

"Don't matter if he's crawled off into the woods," Diehl insisted. "He can just die out there. I need a couple men to attack the big stone house, my old house. Ike Hawkins, the one-legged deputy, and his family are squattin' there." Diehl eyed the gunmen behind Jenkins, then returned Jenkins's stare.

Jenkins leaned back and looked around the circle. "You ain't got any gunmen," he drawled. "I guess you want mine."

Diehl only nodded. Jenkins's stare was making him nervous.

Jenkins scowled, but that was just for show. This was headed the way he wanted it to go. He jerked his thumb at his two new men. "You can borrow Bryce and Shorty for a couple days. I'll take Boots."

Diehl's head came up sharply. "Whaddya want him for?" he demanded. He struggled to hold Jenkin's stare.

Jenkins fished around in his pocket, came out with a toothpick, and made a clucking noise when he stuck it in his mouth. "When you get them old deputies rounded up," he mumbled around the toothpick, "I'm gonna convince the town they need themselves a new sheriff. Boots can help convince 'em."

Diehl dropped his gaze and nodded. "How long do you need Boots?" he asked.

Jenkins shifted the toothpick to the other side of his

mouth. "That depends," he answered, "on how long it takes you to get those deputies out of my way."

———

Jenkins spent the day looking things over in the town of Fredericksburg. Ike Hawkins, the deputy with the wooden leg, stayed at the sheriff's office most of the day, but he moved inside and out, staring down the street, probably wondering what had happened to Boone, the other deputy.

After keeping an eye on the sheriff's office during the morning, he moved among the saloons on Main Street during the afternoon, splitting up and sending Boots to watch and listen, being careful to never be seen in the same place as Boots at the same time.

There wasn't much to be learned at the saloon. People weren't talking about holdups or anything that told Jenkins they were worried about having no sheriff around town. Then again, Boone had only been missing for about a day and a half so far. Things could change.

At the second saloon, Jenkins struck pay dirt when a man came in wearing a black top hat and some other fancy duds. Jenkins heard the barkeep call the guy *Mayor Hall.*

Jenkins nursed his beer and watched the mayor out of the corner of his eye. When he saw his chance, he moved to the mayor's table, lifted his hat, and slid into an empty chair across the table.

"Mayor," he said smoothly. "My name is Logan, Clint Logan," he continued, making up the name on the spot. "I just wanted to meet you. I'm new in town, come down here from Colorado way, where I just done some prospecting, some sheriffing, whatever it took to make my way. If there's anything I can do for you, just let me know."

The mayor was looking at him, just a tad suspicious if Jenkins read the cards right, but there was a spark of interest when he mentioned being a sheriff.

"Help me to do what?" Hall finally asked.

"Oh, I'm handy at a lot of things," Jenkins said vaguely. "If your sheriff needs a deputy or if you need a grave dug on Boot Hill, you can call on me. I'm at the boardinghouse across the street."

Hall nodded and downed the rest of his beer. Jenkins knew he had pushed this far enough. The only thing he needed to do was plant a seed. He had done that. He took his beer and left the mayor in peace.

———

Virgil Diehl stormed back into the cabin where he had shot Boone just about a day ago. There was nobody home. Diehl emerged and stood in front of the door, slapping the wall of the cabin in frustration. It wasn't so much that he had expected to find Boone in here, but where had the man gone? Or the woman, for that matter?

Bryce and Shorty watched him silently. When Diehl wheeled and went back to re-examine the footprints at the top of the rise behind the cabin, Bryce rolled his eyes. This ground had been covered twice. There were tracks coming and going. They led to the cabin at one end and down into the cattle pasture below on the other end. There was no blood on that trail.

Diehl came back to stare at the tracks left by a buggy leading from the cabin out toward the road. They had tried following this trail already, but an overnight shower had wiped out the trail after a hundred yards.

Finally, Diehl turned and led his horse down the rise in back of the cabin. When they reached the pasture below, he knew the way to the big stone house. He followed a faint path cautiously. Maybe Boone was there. Diehl needed to attack that house and take the Hawkins family prisoner before morning. He had promised Jenkins, and a little voice told him he didn't want to disappoint Jenkins.

By late afternoon, the three of them had formed a semi-circle in the trees at the edge of the stone house. An hour later, Ike Hawkins rode in, dismounted, and used his crutch to limp into the cabin. Diehl watched for another hour and saw no more activity either coming or going.

Staying on his belly and worming his way toward the others, Diehl gave both of the gunhands the same message.

"Get some shut-eye. We'll attack in the morning."

———

Julia went into a huddle with her father as soon as he came through the door. She told him about the attack on Boone, and how she had taken Boone and Alice to the cabin on the far edge of the property. Ike nodded once, and he was familiar with the cabin.

When Julia finished talking, Ike rubbed his jaw slowly, then rose and hollered for his oldest son, Pete, to come in.

When Pete arrived, Ike rose and walked to the corner of the room. He picked up a shotgun and a Winchester, keeping the rifle for himself and giving the shotgun to his son. Not seeing Julia's rifle in its normal place, he turned and raised an eyebrow.

"On my horse," Julia answered. "He's saddled and ready to go. I've got him staked out in the trees behind the house."

"Good idea," Ike rumbled. He returned to his seat and relayed Julia's story to Pete. "You an' me," he said to Pete, "take turns on watch from now on." He turned to Julia. "You help Boone and Alice, and if anything happens here, your job is to go find Jake and bring him back."

Julia nodded once, rose silently and slipped out the back door of the house, making her way to her horse. She pulled the horse back farther into the woods and made herself comfortable on her blankets beneath an oak tree. Unable to sleep, she rose before daybreak and started for Boone's cabin.

CHAPTER 16

THE STONE HOUSE

The road home from Ft. Worth was the same one I'd traveled on the way up, but it just seemed to take longer on the way home. I wondered if I should have taken the time to show Hardy and Hostler some of the sights before we left. There was talk of a new streetcar going in and a few other things happening, but they'd assured me they wanted to get going. I guess neither of them was cut out for the big city, either.

About two days down the road, we made camp for the night, managed to eat the dinner Hostler cooked for us, and were getting ready to turn in. Hardy came over and sat down, and I could tell he wanted to talk.

"So," he said, slow to get going, "you think maybe I could work as your deputy for a while? If Boone wants to retire, I mean."

"Sure," I answered. "I'd be glad to have you. If Julia has her way, I might want to hang it up too, and you could run for sheriff yourself after a while."

Hardy sat back and let a grin spread slowly over his face. When a snore sounded from the other side of the log, he glanced over at Hostler. "And maybe Hostler could work on your ranch for a while?" he asked. "He might make a good deputy someday himself."

I hadn't thought about that, but Hostler was a man to be reckoned with, himself. "Sure, maybe," I said. Another snore rumbled from the other side of the log. "He'll be sleeping in the bunkhouse, though," I added.

Hardy chuckled, then turned serious after a moment. "What do I need to learn?" he asked. "I've been in the Army all this time..."

"Nothing much you can't pick up as a deputy," I promised. "You know how to deal with people, you can be tough when you need to be. Anything in particular you're worried about?"

Hardy shrugged. "I can use my Winchester with the best of 'em," he said. He glanced at the Navy Colt laying in the ground beside him. "I've practiced a fair amount with the pistol," he said. "I can hit what I aim at, but I've never much had to defend myself with it."

"I can help," I said. "Main thing is to hit what you aim at. You can practice on the draw and all, but when it comes to somebody standing in front of you and drawing on you, main thing is to aim for the center of him and make your shot count."

Hardy thought that over, nodding his head slowly. "Hopefully," he said finally, "that don't happen anytime real soon."

I nodded, stood and kicked some dirt over the small fire we had built. "Maybe, with a little luck," I said, "it won't come to that for you at all."

———

Ike Hawkins sat in the shadows at the corner of his front porch, watching the first faint streaks of dawn filtering through the trees. He loved this ranch and his family more than anything he'd ever known in life or ever would know. He'd come through the War Between the States and had come home with one leg, but he had brought his family here and given them all a good life. He would protect this with his life.

Ike had alternated shifts on watch with his son Pete during the night. This final shift was his, and then he would get some sleep. He shifted angrily in his chair, remembering his talk with Julia last night. The news that Virgil Diehl was back in town couldn't be anything but bad news.

He had known men like Diehl before. He was a very small man inside who thought he was a big man. That made him dangerous, because he was always trying to prove himself, always trying to make others look up to him. When that didn't work, he did crazy things to make himself look like a big man. Dangerous things.

Ike thought he'd seen motion out of the corner of his eye. He leaned forward just a little, staying in the shadows of the porch, searching the trees in front of him. He eased back the hammer on his Winchester but stayed stock still otherwise, his eyes roaming back and forth, trying to pick up that movement again.

Finally, Ike relaxed. Maybe he'd been out on this porch so long he had started to imagine things. The light from the east was growing, and he wouldn't be in shadow much longer if he stayed where he was. Ike eased the hammer down on his Winchester, scanned the woods one last time, and moved to get up from his chair.

His wooden leg was always a problem when he stood

up, and being out here in this chair most of the night wasn't helping things. He wasn't a young man anymore, Ike reminded himself. He put his free hand on the arm of the chair, holding the Winchester with the other, and pushed himself up.

That first step was always a tricky one, what with the bad leg and all, and Ike stumbled just a bit when he took his first step, bending and reaching down for the arm of the chair again to steady himself. As it turned out, that stumble saved his life.

———

Diehl had given himself the best spot of the three of them, staked out in the woods in front of the stone house. He was behind a fallen log with some thick underbrush around him. His gun barrel was partly covered by some leaves and twigs, and he was lined up on the front porch.

Diehl had lived in that house. He'd had that house built! McCabe and Boone had worked some kind of trick with the banker to get that house from him. The bank was lucky they'd gotten any payments from him at all. Diehl felt a familiar flush of anger, and the heat was creeping up from his neck. He forced himself to calm down.

Diehl concentrated on the porch again, waiting for the dawn to give him a target. He knew that the porch had a pretty good field of fire over these trees where they were hidden. If he were Hawkins, he would be on that porch, just waiting for somebody to show themselves. Diehl laughed, giving off a growling rumble in the underbrush.

"Not a chance, old man," Diehl mumbled. "I'm gonna see you first."

Now, he could see movement on the porch. The old man was in a chair at the back corner. Diehl grinned and sighted down the barrel. The fool had stayed a little too long. There was a shadow back there in that corner, and it was moving. Diehl aimed at the center upper-half of the shadow. He'd never killed a man before, and he wasn't sure he wanted to do that now. What he wanted was to be able tell people later on he had killed a man.

Diehl had his sights on that shadow, staring down the barrel. He took a deep breath and released it slowly, squeezing the trigger. He heard the smack of the bullet into the stone wall, but there was nothing else.

Diehl rose slightly and stared at the porch. Somehow, he seemed to have missed. He dropped and sighted down the barrel again, firing a second and third shots into the corner of that porch. Nothing. No movement, no sound.

Suddenly, he heard a shot from the porch, and a bullet exploded into the log in front of him. Splinters flew from the old log, some of them gouging his cheek. Diehl rolled over, cursing loudly, and two more shots followed the first, both of them scary close.

Diehl clapped his hand over his mouth and forced himself to lie still. How had the old man come so close? How could he have known? Then he knew how the old coot had come so close...muzzle flash. It was dark enough he'd seen the muzzle flash on those second and third shots.

Diehl cursed again, but quietly this time. He moved a little way down the log and sighted on the porch again. He jumped suddenly when Shorty, in the woods to his left, opened up with shot after shot at the porch.

Fool! That was Diehl's first thought. The fool didn't even have a clean shot at the porch from over there. Diehl said nothing and lay quietly behind the log. Might as well let that idiot draw the fire for a while. The old coot on the porch could shoot.

Shorty fired two more shots from his position on Diehl's left. An answering shot ripped through the leaves and twigs. Shorty dropped his rifle, howled, and fell to the ground. He lay quietly for a while, then Diehl could hear the sounds of Shorty crawling toward his position.

"Fool!" Diehl hissed. "Stay where you are!"

"I'm hit," came a low moan in response. "Got me in the shoulder. How'd that old fossil even find me?"

"Muzzle flash, you fool," Diehl growled. "Hold your position!" he repeated.

"I need help," Shorty moaned.

"You're drawing the fire over here," Diehl warned. Another shot ripped through the bushes above his head. "If you get any closer, I'll shoot you myself!"

———

Ike had dropped to the porch floor when the first shot tore open the morning calm. He had crawled to the front door, using the porch railing for a small amount of cover. He lay flat on the porch and sighted under the railing. When he saw the muzzle flash, he held low and fired his first shot. When he heard the cursing coming from the trees, he smiled grimly to himself and used the moment to crawl into the stone house.

Staying on hands and knees, he moved to the front window and peered over the sill. Somebody was firing blindly at the front porch. Ike raised himself slightly, balanced his Winchester on the sill and fired at the muzzle flashes. He heard a cry from the woods. He'd at least winged somebody out there.

"Ike?" His wife Jeanne was on her knees, peeking around a corner from the back bedroom. "What do you want me to do?"

"Get the rifles by the back porch," he answered. "Give one to Pete. Keep one for yourself. Isaac can...reload. There's a pistol or two back there. You and Pete can use the pistols when Isaac reloads."

He heard Jeanne crawling away, moving toward the rifles at the back. He risked another look out the window. It was quiet for the moment, so he moved to the other window in the front room. Still nothing out there.

Ike leaned against the wall and reloaded. He pulled the ammo box from his jacket pocket and looked inside in the dim light. Ammo could be a problem for them. He peered out the window again. He knew there was one man on his right he'd probably wounded. One in the middle he'd probably just scared. But he was pretty sure there was a third man on the left who had fired only once. That one worried him.

Jeanne crawled into the front room. She had an old Spencer with her. Multiple shots rang out from the bedroom on the left, and Ike turned toward Jeanne. "Tell Pete to save his ammo," Ike whispered. "Tell him not to shoot unless he's sure he sees something."

More shots rang out as Jeanne crawled away. Ike leaned against the wall, shaking his head. At this rate, they would be out of ammo in just a few minutes. He tried to remember where they had stored the extra bullets.

Pete knelt at his bedroom window, firing into the woods with his Winchester. His little brother Isaac was laying on the floor beside him. He thought his heart was pounding just as loudly as the rifle. He was sure he had seen something out there...

"Pete!"

It was his mother. He turned to see her crawling into his room. A single shot sounded, and a bullet tore through the room and struck the back wall.

His mother lay on the floor for a moment, then raised her head. "Save your ammunition! Your father says to only shoot if you're sure you can see your target!"

Pete nodded, and she crawled back toward the front room. He pushed himself off the floor and laid a hand on the window sill. He was surprised to see how much that hand was shaking.

There! Maybe that was something. Pete fired twice, then dropped to the floor, waiting. There was no answering shot. He looked into the box of ammunition next to him on the floor. He had only five bullets left.

Pete turned to his little brother. "You've got to get us more ammo, Isaac," he said.

Isaac stared at him. "Are you crazy?" he blurted. "Where? Where is there any more ammo? I can't get out to the barn."

Pete shook his head. "The root cellar," he said. "Just a few feet out the back door. I put about three boxes in the root cellar. Pa said to keep some close to hand, but hide it, like. You can crawl out the back door and go into the root cellar. You got to go now!"

Isaac stared at his brother, but turned and started

crawling toward the back door. He knew just where those boxes of ammo were. Maybe he could get there and back before anybody started shooting from behind the house.

Isaac reached the back door and inched it open soundlessly. He dropped down flat on the floor and inched forward, looking in all directions. There was nothing moving. All was quiet. Isaac inched out the door and crawled down the three steps. He started crawling toward the root cellar, but a little voice inside him screamed to get out there, get the ammo, and get back.

He rose, hunched over, and ran for the root cellar, yanking the door over and ducking down as he hurried down the steps. He left the door open and lay on the ground above him. He needed that little bit of early morning light it would give him.

Inside the root cellar, he had just enough light to inch to his left. He reached out and found the wall, then dropped to his knees and searched with both hands. There! He found some boxes and pulled them out to get a little better light.

Isaac grabbed three boxes of Winchester ammo and one box for his father's pistol. He couldn't do anything about his mother's Spencer. There was no ammunition for it down here. Holding the boxes in both hands, he came to the foot of the stairs and gathered his breath. He would go straight up the stairs and run to the house. Never mind closing the root cellar door.

Isaac raced up the stairs, his hopes rising as he reached the top step. Maybe, he thought, this was going to work.

————

Bryce stayed where he was, shaking his head in disgust when the gunfire erupted to his left. Why didn't the fools just hold up a sign and beg Hawkins to shoot them? Bryce had taken only one shot. After Diehl had taken his first shot, Bryce had spotted the old man moving toward the door. He had fired at Hawkins only once. The old man's uneven gait on the wooden leg had thrown him off a little.

With any luck, Bryce thought, the defenders in the cabin still didn't know about him out here on the edge. That's the way he preferred it. Diehl and Shorty could draw all the fire they wanted. Bryce preferred to wait things out.

He sat and studied the layout of the stone house. Diehl hadn't told them anything about the ground in back of the house. Bryce moved a little to his right, trying to see the lay of the land at the side of the house. A volley of shots erupted from a new spot in the stone house. Somebody was firing from a window over on Bryce's side.

He sat and waited it out. Whoever it was, he was firing blindly. Sooner or later, he would either run out of ammo and get tired of shooting without a target.

The firing stopped abruptly. Bryce stayed put, waiting to see if there would be a fresh volley. When there wasn't, he began moving, slowly and low to the ground. He wanted to flank the house on the right side and see if they were vulnerable from the side or in back.

After a few minutes, Bryce began to flank the house on the right, and he began moving a little faster. Whoever was firing from that window wouldn't be able to see him now. Bryce found no entry or point of attack on the side of the house, so he kept moving around to the back, happy he still had cover from the oak trees.

When he reached the back, he froze. There was movement from the back of the house. Bryce hunched down and watched. After a minute or two, he could see a young boy creeping from the back door and moving into the yard. After another moment, Bryce could see something being lifted and set aside on the ground.

A thin smile crossed his face. It was a root cellar. The kid had gone into the root cellar for some reason. Bryce had no intention of shooting the kid, but he would make a great hostage. He stood and covered the ground quickly to the root cellar. When the kid's head showed, climbing out of the cellar, Bryce pulled his Colt .45 and thumbed the hammer back.

"Don't move and don't make a noise, kid," he growled softly. "You'll live longer that way."

The kid was canny. Bryce had to give him credit for that. He froze in his tracks and nodded his head up and down slowly. Bryce pulled the boxes from his hand, glanced at them, and tossed them back in the cellar. Then he pulled the kerchief from around his neck and stuffed it in the kid's mouth. After that, he proceeded to drag the boy back into the cover of the trees.

CHAPTER 17

SENDING WORD

Ike found a position that allowed him to stretch out his bad leg while he kept watch through the front room window. Jeanne fired a shot from the other window once in a while just to keep them guessing, but they were dangerously low on ammunition. The firing from the trees in front of them had all but stopped. Ike was still worried there might be someone on his far left. What was that guy doing?

His answer came just a minute later. A voice sounded from off on the left edge.

"Hawkins! I've got your boy! Put down your guns and come out with your hands in the air. All of you!"

Seconds later, Pete crawled into the living room. "They've got Isaac," he mumbled. Tears were starting down his cheeks. "It's my fault. I sent him out the back door to get ammo from the root cellar. I didn't think there was anybody back there." Pete slumped back against the wall and stared at his father.

Ike took only a second to think it over. "Okay, son, we'll figger this out. For now, we've got to do like he says and come out." He paused for just a moment longer. "You for sure saw somebody out there with Isaac?"

Pete nodded miserably.

Ike boosted himself to his feet, grimacing from the pain it caused him. "Me first," he said. "Jeanne, you behind me, and Pete last. Everybody keeps their hands in the air, no matter what."

Ike opened the door and stepped outside. As the three of them moved out to the porch, a man emerging from the trees to their left caught their attention. He was pushing Isaac in front of him. Isaac had a kerchief stuffed in his mouth as a gag, and his hands appeared to be tied behind his back. Ike didn't recognize the man behind him.

A man stood up from the underbrush in front of them, and Virgil Diehl stepped out. He held his sleeve up to his cheek, and Ike could see there was blood on Diehl's face.

Isaac and his captor reached the porch first, then Diehl. Ike stared at Diehl.

"Come to steal your house back?" Ike asked.

Diehl drew his fist back to punch Ike, but the man who had taken Isaac captive reached over and grabbed the fist. Diehl cursed and whirled to face the man. They stared at each other. Diehl backed down first. Ike made a mental note. Diehl might think he's in charge, Ike thought, but the other guy is the one to be reckoned with.

The underbrush rustled to the right, and a third man came out. His shirt was bloody, and he held a hand to his left shoulder. He stumbled a time or two as he came forward. His face was pale.

Isaac's captor released the boy. Diehl shoved Isaac forward. "Everybody inside," he ordered.

All of them shuffled into the living room. Diehl pointed at Jeanne. "Take Shorty, here, out to the kitchen and attend to that shoulder," he ordered her. She took the injured man away.

Diehl ordered the remaining three of the Hawkins family to sit, braced against the wall. "This is my house again," he informed them. "This is my ranch again and you'll be my guests for a while." He looked around the room, then pointed his rifle at Ike.

"Where's the girl?" he demanded. "Where's your daughter?"

Ike stared at him, thinking quickly. He had to be truthful to the extent of what Diehl already knew.

"Haven't seen her in a couple days," he answered. "She went over to see Boone and his wife in their cabin up yonder. Haven't seen her since."

Diehl stared at him, trying to decide if he believed Hawkins. He knew the girl had been at Boone's cabin when they attacked it. He decided Hawkins could be telling the truth.

"Where's McCabe?" he asked.

"Haven't seen him in weeks," Ike answered truthfully. "He went up north with Leander McNelly and some Rangers."

Diehl blinked several times, then paced back and forth in the room.

He knew that, Ike thought—he already knew McCabe had been up north. He filed that little piece of information away and waited.

Diehl whirled abruptly and pointed at the bigger of his gunhands. "Bryce, watch 'em. I'm gonna check on Shorty."

Ike watched Diehl walk away. We just need a little

time, he thought. Julia had almost certainly made it over to Boone's shack, and they would work on a way to get McCabe back into town. They just needed a little time.

———

Julia heard the gunshots just as she reached the line cabin where Boone and Alice were hiding. She dismounted, heard the shots, then spun back around and grabbed the reins.

"No!" It was Boone, standing at the door of the line cabin with the help of some sort of makeshift crutch. Alice was framed in the doorway behind him.

"You can't get there in time," Boone said. "Come on into the cabin and we'll figger out what to do. It won't do us no good if you go ridin' back and get yourself captured. Ike's savvy. He'll deal with it."

Julia slowly let go of the reins and trudged into the line cabin, glancing over her shoulder when a fresh volley of firing started at the ranch house.

Boone stood in the doorway, listening, then slowly pushed the door shut. There was some food on a plate in the corner. Julia shook her head when Alice offered the food.

Boone eased himself down on the mattress, supporting himself with the crutch with one hand and holding Alice's arm with the other. He grimaced when he dropped the last foot onto the mattress. Julia's secret hope that Boone could come back to the ranch with her evaporated when she saw his condition.

Boone looked across the room at Julia. "Any chance somebody saw you and follered you out here?"

Julia shook her head emphatically. "I left before they

came, and I checked my back trail all the way," she assured him. "They don't know about this place and they don't know where I am. Or you."

Boone stroked his chin. "Good," he muttered. "Good." He looked over at Alice, then back at Julia. "Best way we can help your family is to get hold of Jake and get him back here. I know you want to go back over to the house, but I'm all stove up and you're outnumbered. We've got to get Jake."

Julia waited, then nodded. "Dad said the same," she agreed. "He told me if anything happens, find Jake and get him back here." She blew out a long breath. "I don't know how to reach him," she said miserably. "I sent a telegram to the hotel he was planning to use in Ft. Worth, but he didn't answer. If he's still at the Palo Duro Canyon, I can't reach him. If he's on the way home, I don't know how to get in touch." She stopped, frustrated, and stared at the floor. "What if they ambush him on the way home?" she added.

Boone slumped a bit on the mattress and went back to stroking his chin. Suddenly, he sat up and snapped his fingers. "On the way home," he muttered.

"On the way home," he repeated. "He'll ride through Waco on the way home."

Julia nodded, puzzled, and watched Boone.

"There's a sheriff in Waco, helped us out a while back," Boone explained. "It's real likely Jake will look him up or at least run into him when he goes through Waco. We got to get a telegram to him." He stared at the ceiling, scratching his chin. He snapped his fingers again. "Waters, that's his name. Sheriff Waters. We got to get a telegram to him."

Julia started to her feet, feeling hope for the first time

in a while. "I'll go now. I'll take the long way around the ranch."

"No." Boone shook his head. "They might have somebody staking out the town, too, and they might know you. Got to be somebody they don't know."

Julia slumped back to the floor. There was no chance Boone was in shape for a ride to town, and it was just as likely they knew him, too. Slowly, Julia and Boone both swung their heads to look at Alice.

She reached for a hat and tied it on. "I'll do it," she said simply.

Julia held the cabin door open. "Take my horse," she said. "He's still saddled." She followed Alice outside. "I brought a pack of food," she said. "I'll bring that inside for Boone."

———

"Logan! Clint Logan!"

Jenkins was intent on his breakfast at the Main Street Café in Fredericksburg, and it took him a moment to recognize his latest fake name. He looked up to see a faintly familiar face crossing the room, and it came together for him.

"Mayor Hall!" Jenkins rose, pointed at the empty chair across the table, and took a seat again. Clint Logan, he remembered, was the name he'd given Hall when he asked the mayor what he could do to help the town. He would have to remember that name.

The mayor took a seat and came right to the point. "We haven't seen the sheriff in over three weeks, and now we can't seem to find either deputy. We sent a man out and neither of them seems to be home." Mayor Hall frowned. "Strangest thing, about those deputies."

Jenkins remembered to paste on a surprised/concerned look. This meant Diehl was right on schedule, getting the two old deputies out of the way. He sat back and waited for what else the mayor had to say.

"I don't know if you had much plan to stick around town for long," Hall started, glancing up to see how he was doing.

"What can I do?" Jenkins asked smoothly. This was going better than he could have ever expected.

"I'm hopin', subject to the town council approving things, of course, that you'll serve as our temporary mayor, kinda keep a lid on things for us until we can locate the deputies, an' maybe until our sheriff, McCabe, gets back in town. You know McCabe?" he asked as an afterthought.

"Never met him," Jenkins lied smoothly. He fiddled with his coffee cup and pretended to be making a tough decision.

"D'you think the council will agree with you?" he asked abruptly.

Hall scratched his ear and shrugged. "Probly," he answered, continuing to think out loud. "We've got a saloon owner, an' he'll just want to keep it peaceful. Same for the feed store owner. Sam the barber, he don't much care one way or the other. Only one might not agree is Hayes, the banker. He's kinda partial to McCabe and the Hawkins clan. We could outvote him, though."

Jenkins nodded thoughtfully and drained the last of his coffee. "Why don't you get the council together, Mayor?" he suggested. "Maybe at the sheriff's office at

12:00? Would that work? I could talk to them after you do."

"Good idea!" Hall rose and stuck out his hand. "Just to keep the lid on the place till we can figger out what's what."

Jenkins rose and shook his hand, then settled back into his chair. He needed Boots to go over and pay this banker a visit before the meeting. He looked around, suddenly angry. Where was Boots? Still snoring in his bed, probably. Jenkins left a coin on the table and marched out of the café. Time for Boots to earn his money. Well, time to earn Diehl's money, he corrected himself. This was going to work out.

Jenkins could make himself a lot of money in Fredericksburg. And he would do it at Jake McCabe's expense. That was the best part.

———

Alice rode quickly, bypassing the Hawkins ranch on her ride into town. She was looking for faces she didn't recognize as she pulled up in front of the telegraph office. Boone was worried that Diehl had some people in town as well as at the ranch. All the faces she saw looked familiar, but it didn't make her feel much better.

She dismounted and tied Julia's horse to the railing. As she stepped up to enter the telegraph office, she saw several men entering the sheriff's office, just down the street. She stepped back and stopped a man passing by her.

"What's going on over there?" she asked, making her voice as casual as possible.

The man stopped and tipped his hat. "Meeting of the

council, ma'am, that's what I hear," he replied. "Our sheriff's been gone a while and we ain't seen the deputies in a while, neither. Mayor wants to get somebody in there, temporary-like, until we get our sheriff and deputies back." He replaced his hat on his head and sauntered off.

Alice turned and hurried into the telegraph office. She glanced around and saw no one else in the office besides the clerk. She grabbed a pencil and piece of paper and hurried to write her message.

For Jake McCabe:

Bandits have attacked the ranch. Stop

We think it might be Virgil Diehl. Stop

F'Burg is voting on new temp sheriff. Stop

Please meet Julia on road north of town soonest. Be careful. Stop

Boone/Alice.

She handed the message to the clerk and watched his eyebrows shoot up in astonishment when he read it.

"Is this true?" he asked. "Why don't you talk to the mayor?"

"The mayor doesn't know me, and I don't know him," she answered quickly. "I need you to send this right now to Sheriff Waters in Waco. He'll get help for us."

The clerk nodded, his fingers drumming nervously on the countertop. He nodded again, went over, and sent the message. He returned the paper to Julia. She handed it back.

"Burn it," she said. "I'd suggest you burn your copy of the message, too. And don't tell anybody else about it."

"Yes, ma'am." The clerk tossed both pieces of paper into a small fireplace at the back of the store.

Alice moved toward the door, but the clerk stopped her. "Do you live near Julia McCabe?" he asked.

Alice turned back and nodded. The clerk passed a telegram to her. It had come in two days ago. Alice moved outside and scanned the message. Jake McCabe was on his way home. He had left Ft. Worth after sending the telegram.

Alice hesitated when she reached her horse, wondering if she should wait to find out what would happen at the meeting in the sheriff's office. She decided against it and rode quickly out of town.

———

Mark Hayes, Fredericksburg town councilman, leaned forward in the uncomfortable wooden chair in the sheriff's office. Mayor Hall had called a meeting to discuss installing a temporary sheriff. Hall had explained Sheriff McCabe had been gone *for a while*, and the two deputies couldn't be found.

Hayes was troubled by what he was hearing at the meeting, but he was even more troubled by what had happened while he was walking to the meeting just a few minutes ago.

As he had turned the corner, coming from the bank to the sheriff's office, a huge, bearded man in a dirty vest had pushed away from the wall to block Hayes's path.

"Heard you're headed for a meetin' at the sheriff's office," the man had rumbled.

Hayes had glanced at the man and attempted to step

around him. The man had moved surprisingly quickly to block his path again.

"Don't like bein' ignored," he'd said, leaning in.

"Just trying to take care of some business," Hayes had said, leaning away from the foul-smelling breath.

"Town like this needs to have a sheriff here in town, lookin' after things, don'tcha think?" The man had checked over his shoulder to see if they were being watched.

"We a have a sheriff who does that," Hayes said, trying to pass again.

The man had grabbed his arm and squeezed until Hayes had winced. "You don't wanna ignore me," he advised. "It would be good for ever'body if you vote for the new sheriff."

Hayes leaned back and stared at him. "We have a sheriff. Are you threatening me?"

A few people turned the corner and walked in their direction. The man let go, but leaned in as Hayes passed him.

"You an' me, we might have to meet up again after the meetin'," he said. "You don't want that."

Hayes forced himself to concentrate on what was happening now in the meeting. Mayor Hall had told them neither the sheriff nor the deputies could be found, and he was proposing putting in a temporary sheriff, a man named Clint Logan, who claimed to have experience at this, until the sheriff or the deputies showed up.

Hayes heard the door to the office open and close. He looked around to see the man who had stopped him in the street. The man walked over and leaned against the wall next to Hayes. He folded his arms and said nothing.

Hall called on Earl Cooper, owner of the Main Street

Saloon, who stood and said he was all for keeping things peaceful so he could make some money. "Don't need no brawls or shootin'," he said. He would welcome the new sheriff.

The other two councilmen shrugged, nodded, and said nothing. Hayes stood, and the man next to him came off the wall. Hayes ignored him.

"Jake McCabe has always been here for us," he pointed out. "And deputies Boone and Hawkins are reliable men, too. Why don't we just wait for a few days and make another effort to find them? Let's send a telegram to the Texas Rangers and ask for their help."

Clint Logan stood. Hayes had a feeling that wasn't his real name. "Mayor Hall, and Mr. Hayes," he said smoothly. "That's the very first thing I'll do. I'll get in touch with the Rangers and I'll send a man to find the deputies. We'll get this cleared up right away."

Hall nodded in satisfaction, then waved a hand to stop Hayes from speaking again. "Let's take a vote," he said. The town council voted four to one in favor of hiring Clint Logan as sheriff until Jake McCabe could be found.

Hayes shook his head in frustration and walked out, feeling the stranger's eyes on his back all the way.

Two blocks down the street, he turned the corner and heard footsteps right behind him. Wheeling around to see who was following, he never got a chance to say a word. A huge right fist smashed into his stomach, knocking him to the ground. Hayes's head bounced off the ground and he fell heavily on his back. He barely felt it when a heavy boot kicked him in the ribs after he was down. He passed out immediately.

CHAPTER 18

MOVING IN

Alice was greeted by Julia outside the line cabin. Alice saw the Winchester propped against the wall by the door. Julia remained outside for a few minutes after Alice went inside. Finally, satisfied that Alice hadn't been followed, she went inside and listened to Alice's update on things in Fredericksburg.

Boone laid against the back wall of the cabin and digested what Alice said about the meeting to appoint a new sheriff in Fredericksburg. Boone shifted the leg with the gunshot wound and winced, but Julia thought his color was better. Jake had always described Boone as a *tough old bird*. Now she could see why.

"There was a feller who get hisself elected sheriff over in Fredericksburg," Boone observed. "Not too long ago. He was runnin' some road agents, robbing stages and such near town, and demanding payments from business folks. Went by the name of Abe Richards then, but he could be callin' hisself just about anything now."

Julia waited while Boone thought things through.

Finally, he grabbed his crutch and stood, hobbling out to the door of the line cabin.

"Two things we gotta do," he told Julia. "One thing Alice and me can do, and the other you'll have to do."

"Alice got the telegram off. Probly just in time. This bogus sheriff is gonna shut off the telegraph pretty soon. We'll have to assume the one Alice already sent will get through to Jake in Waco. Julia, you've got to meet him on the road north of town, like the telegram said. If he don't show up in a couple days, we'll have to try to get a message to the Rangers over in Austin."

Julia nodded. "What are you doing to do?" she asked. "You can barely get around."

Boone pointed at the buggy, still standing in back of the cabin. "You can get me over to a spot where I can watch the stone house," he said. He lifted a pair of field glasses off a hook on the wall. Jake's gonna need to know how many of them varmints are over there, an' what's going on. I'm gonna scout things out for him. You meet him on the road, then bring him to where I'm watching."

Julia looked at Boone doubtfully, then looked over at Alice, who was already packing up some food and supplies. She looked up at Julia. "He'll do it with or without us," she said. "He's got a head that's harder than a rock. We might as well help him."

Julia helped Boone out to the buggy and made him comfortable. Alice followed with food, water, and rags to keep the gunshot wound clean. They pulled away from the line cabin, taking a long route around the stone house and then on foot through the woods until Boone pronounced himself satisfied with a lookout spot to the side of the house, sixty or seventy yards away and screened by a thick stand of post oaks.

Both women helped him settle down on a blanket, positioning him behind a fallen tree and leaving his rifle handy. Julia watched as Alice settled down to tend Boone's wound. "I'll be back in two days, with or without Jake," she told them. Then she melted away into the trees.

————

We rode into Waco after three days of hard riding. I'd been worried Hardy and Hostler might be needin' a stopover and a good night's sleep by the time we got here, but I forgot they were Army boys through and through. They were happy if I bought 'em a good breakfast at the café. I knew that would cost me.

I ate my fill and settled down for a second cup of coffee while Hardy and Hostler went at it. I was pretty sure they had ordered everything on the menu. Maybe twice for some of 'em. Hardy finally threw in the towel, but Hostler kept going.

Just then, the door swung open, and an old friend walked in. Sheriff Waters had been with me, along with McNelly, when we attacked an outlaw fort up in No Man's Land. Come to think of it, Hardy and Hostler had both been there too. I stood and waved at Waters to take a seat.

"I'd buy you breakfast," I told him, "But these two done cleaned me out."

Waters waved a hand in the air and sat down. "Already ate," he said. He reached into this shirt pocket and pulled out a piece of paper. "Been looking for you," he said. "Telegram came in for you only about a half hour ago." He pushed the paper over to me.

I opened the telegram. I glanced at the bottom first, wondering who would try to get hold of me here. I saw it came from Boone and Alice, and a sick feeling shot through me. I read the message, then read it again. I expect I went white, because they were all staring at me when I looked up.

"Got trouble at home," I told them. "We got to get down to Fredericksburg the fastest way we can." I looked at Waters.

"Fastest way would be to take the Houston and Texas Central Railroad spur to Bremond, then take another train to Austin." He pulled a watch out of his pocket and looked. "You can get there today," he said. "Then you maybe got a two-day hard ride to Fredericksburg."

I jumped up and ran outside. They all followed. We mounted up and rode to the station. Our luck was good. The next train to Bremond left in a half hour. We got the horses loaded. Waters asked me what else he could do, and I thought about it.

"You could send a telegram to Trey Stanton, Ranger in Austin," I said. "I don't know if he's up and around yet, but ask him to meet me at the train station tonight, or send somebody I can trust if he can't make it. We could use a spare horse apiece if he can manage it."

Waters shook my hand. "Done," he said. We jumped aboard and the train moved off. I filled in Hardy and Hostler on what I knew as we rode. I knew I could never sleep, but advised them to get some shut-eye if they could. We were several hours away from Austin.

———

Trey Stanton was there when we rolled in. He was a little wobbly on his feet, but looking a lot better than he had after he'd been ambushed a few weeks back. He had three extra horses for us, along with some biscuits and beans, and he wasn't even asking questions.

I filled him in on the telegram I'd just received in Waco. "You're not in shape to ride," I told him, but is there anybody you can send to Fredericksburg in the next day or two? Stanton thought about it for a minute, then a slow grin spread across his face.

"McNelly's due back in town from the canyon tomorrow," he said. "I'll just bet he'd like to get in on this."

I grabbed the lead rope for one of the spare horses and swung aboard mine. "I'll just bet he would," I said. "Tell him I'd be glad to see him if he can come."

With that, we lit out down the road for Fredericksburg. I wanted to find Julia on that road north of town before daybreak if we could do it.

————

We stopped only to switch horses, and to water them when we crossed a stream along the way. Luckily, I had traveled this road many times, and I could find my way through the night. We pushed straight through, and by the time we were only an hour or two ahead of sunrise, I relaxed a little, figuring we were close to meeting up with Julia.

We slowed as we got closer. I'd managed to nod off a few times on the train, but I found the tired feelings dropping away as we got closer. Two days had gone by since Alice had sent that telegram. I wondered what I would find at the ranch, and in my hometown. Palo Duro Canyon seemed like a distant memory now.

A light showed at the side of the road. I lifted my hand and reined in immediately. My hand rested above my Colt, but that was just reflex. No bushwhacker would light up a lantern before he started shooting.

There was a rustle of brush, and Julia stepped out into the road. I swung down and wrapped my arms around her as she came in. We whispered back and forth for a minute, then I turned around and introduced Hardy and Hostler.

"Good," Julia said as she stepped over and hugged them both. "I don't know how many we're facing at the ranch. I thought Jake might be coming by himself, and Boone's laid up."

That was news to me. Julia explained how Boone had been shot at his cabin, and how he was out there now, scouting the place for me. I felt the anger surge up in me as I swung back up onto my horse.

"Is it Diehl?" I asked Julia.

She shrugged. "We think it might be," she answered. "Neither Boone or I got a look at him when he attacked the cabin, but I thought I saw him in town a while back. We don't know how many men he has, but Boone can tell us when I take you to him."

———

Forty-five minutes later we had dismounted and were approaching Boone's camp. I stopped and looked at the eastern sky. "We need to wait another half hour," I told them. I looked at Hardy and Hostler. "I'm sure I don't have to tell you boys about walking up to a campfire in the dark," I said.

Their chuckles told me they knew all about it. "Do you have some kind of signal you arranged with Boone?" I asked Julia. "So he'll know it's you coming in?"

She shook her head. "Sorry, no," she said. "We set all this up in a pretty big hurry and I didn't think of it."

"Okay," I said. "I can do a decent imitation of a dove. "Boone will know it's me."

"And," said Julia, "can Boone *coo* like a dove too?"

I grinned in the dark. "Naw, he's lousy at that, but I can recognize Boone trying to sound like a dove."

We moved forward when the first gray streaks of light filtered in from the east. We stopped every ten yards and I cupped my hands and did my dove call. The third time we stopped, I got an answer.

I could hear Pike Hardy chuckling under his breath behind me. "I see what you mean," he said. "I'm not sure if it's a dove or a tomcat on the prowl."

In another few yards, I could see Boone, with his Winchester laid on top of a log. He waved us in when he saw us. He lit up when he saw Hardy and Hostler.

"I was wondering how old Jake was gonna get all three of 'em," he said. "Now it's all even, and we've got the surprise on our side."

Boone proceeded to lay out for us what he'd seen at the stone house. "Three of 'em, like I said," he told us. "It's Virgil Diehl in there for sure. Two gunhands, one of them's been shot through the shoulder, it looks like. He mostly sits on the porch. Diehl mostly stays inside. The third one looks pretty salty. He comes out to check the perimeter a couple times a day. Goes to the barn early mornings. Mebbe he's feeding the horses."

I glanced at the sky overhead. We had no time to waste. I looked at Pike. "Can you get in the barn and take the salty one by surprise? Right now, I mean, can you get in there with nobody seeing you?"

Hardy stood and picked up his Winchester. "I grew up with the Injuns," he said. "Just watch me."

Pike Hardy moved into the trees. I looked over at Hostler. "We're going in the back door," I told him. "You take the guy with the shot shoulder. I'll take the other." I paused and thought. "There will be four hostages in there," I said. "Ike, the father, has a wooden leg. His wife will be in there, and two boys. Keep a sharp eye out for them."

Hostler met my eye and nodded. He's steady, I thought. These guys won't know what hit them.

———

Pike Hardy knew it was important to get to the barn before the sun was up and people started moving around in the big stone house. He stepped carefully to make as little noise as possible, but mainly, he wanted to get into the barn unnoticed, while there wasn't much light yet, before Diehl's gunhand made his early morning visit. In his experience, people got a lot more cooperative when they were covered with a Winchester up close.

He needed only about five minutes to reach the edge of the tree line. The barn shielded him from being seen from the stone house, so Hardy covered the ground to the back of the barn immediately, then moved to the edge of the barn. He squatted down and looked around the edge. He wasn't yet in view from a window or the front door of the house.

Flattening himself against the side of the barn, Hardy edged down the length of the building. When he reached the front corner, there was nothing for it but to move around the edge and over to the barn door, hoping nobody was watching from the house.

Hardy hunched down and moved to the barn door, avoiding the urge to run. Sudden movement was more likely to catch somebody's eye than slow, steady movement. After what seemed an eternity, waiting for a shot to ring out from the house, he reached the door and slipped into the barn.

There were four horses in stalls inside the barn. Hardy noted that there was no hay in the stalls, meaning somebody would probably come to feed them before long. The fifth stall was empty. Hardy stepped inside and laid his Winchester over the edge, trained on the front door. Now, he would just have to wait.

It was only about ten minutes later that the door to the barn swung open, and a tall, dark-haired man stepped in. Hardy noticed he wore double tied-down pistols, but carried no rifle. The man took three steps into the barn and reached for a hay fork.

Hardy eased back the hammer on his Winchester, creating a surprisingly loud click in the old barn. The man froze where he was, with his right arm partly extended, reaching for the hay fork.

"Good choice," Hardy told him. "You can make this nice and easy now. Just reach down, ever so slow, and pull those smokewagons outta the holsters. Then drop them on the ground."

The man reached first with his left hand, pulling the pistol and dropping it on the ground. Hardy knew what was coming next. The man would have pulled both pistols and dropped them together if he was going to surrender.

He reached for the right-hand gun, easing it gently from the holster. He turned slightly, holding it loosely by the grip, and reached out with it.

"Easy," said Pike Hardy, his finger tightening slightly on the trigger.

The outlaw suddenly snatched up the gun in his fist and dove for the cover of the first stall, trying to take away Hardy's clear shot.

Hardy moved the barrel of the Winchester, aiming slightly lower as he pulled the trigger. The outlaw had crouched for a dive, and was lifting the pistol when Hardy fired. The bullet caught him in the center of his chest. He pitched over onto his back, the pistol clattering onto the floor of the barn.

Hardy waited several seconds, keeping him covered. The pistol was still in reach of the outlaw. When the man didn't move, Hardy eased out from behind the horse stall. One down, he thought, two to go.

———

There wasn't a path to follow through the trees and around to the back of the stone house, but I didn't need one. Even in the dim light of sunrise, I found my way easily. Hostler followed in my footsteps. When we came even with the corner of the house, I raised my hand to call a halt. We would watch for one man to go out to the barn before we came in the back door. I didn't want to be outgunned.

We didn't have long to wait. When a stranger left the house and moved toward the barn, Hostler and I kept going to the back of the house. We would have to count on Pike Hardy taking out the man at the barn. I wasn't really worried about that.

Taking out the first guy turned out to be easy. We had almost reached the back door when somebody came out, headed for the privy out back. He opened his mouth to shout, but Hostler brought down the barrel of his Colt and knocked him cold before he could make any sound. He fell to the ground. There was a bandage around his shoulder.

That left only Virgil Diehl inside. I left Hostler to tie up our new prisoner and eased my way into the house. I could hear voices in the front room, so I moved in that direction on cat feet. I slid up to the end of the hallway and peeked around the corner.

Diehl was standing with his back to me. He was holding his pistol, waving it in the air and talking about how this was going to be his town again. He stopped, pointed the pistol at Jeanne and ordered her to go out to the kitchen and get him some food. She passed without seeing me.

I moved in a little farther, and Ike spotted me. He was sitting across the room from me. His mouth dropped open in surprise, and Diehl started to turn in my direction. Just then, we heard a gunshot out in the barn.

Diehl wheeled and sprung toward the door, but Ike stuck out his good leg and tripped him. Diehl spilled heavily to the floor, losing his grip on the pistol. It skidded toward the door. I stepped into the room, holding my Colt on him.

"Stay right there, Diehl," I told him. I stepped around him, picked up his gun and tossed it away. I holstered my Colt. "Now," I told him, "You can get up."

He got to his knees and started to rise, but something was wrong. I couldn't see one of his hands, and when he looked up, his eyes were lit with a strange excitement. Crazy eyes, I thought. I had seen crazy eyes before, and it was never good.

CHAPTER 19

SETTLING THE SCORE

Virgil Diehl had been nervous ever since he had come back to Fredericksburg. He just didn't like to admit it. They had taken the stone house without much trouble, but there had been no sign of the girl or McCabe. What if the girl had gone to get McCabe and tipped him off?

Plus, he didn't entirely trust Jenkins and his men. He had a feeling Jenkins wanted to be the top dog around here himself. Diehl kept a hideout gun strapped to his ankle, just in case they turned on him. Nobody knew about that hideout gun. It was his ace in the hole.

Diehl paced the living room, barking at Ike Hawkins and his boys. He kept all three of them tied up and left the woman free to cook his food. Diehl turned and ordered her to get him some breakfast.

Just then, there was a shot. It sounded like it came from the barn. Diehl whirled and jumped toward the door, but the old man stuck out his leg and tripped him. Diehl hit the floor hard. His gun skidded away, and then he heard the voice he feared and hated. It was McCabe.

"Get up," McCabe told him. Diehl shielded McCabe's view with one leg while he reached down and took out his hideout gun from the other. A quick glance told him McCabe had holstered his gun. Diehl felt excitement. He felt giddy as he came off the floor and lifted his hideout gun.

Then something went wrong. He felt a tremendous blow to his chest, then another. He tried to pull the trigger, but his hideout gun wasn't pointed at McCabe. It was pointed at the floor. He tried to lift it, but it was incredibly heavy. How could such a small gun be so heavy? Now, he was leaning against the wall. He couldn't remember how he got here. Diehl opened his mouth to say something, but there was blood coming from somewhere.

His feet slid out from under him and he landed on the floor, then pitched over onto his side. This wasn't how it was supposed to turn out...

———

We gathered on the front porch of the stone house to hold a council of war on what our next steps would be. Pike Hardy had gone out to help Boone come into the house. Julia and Alice had made him comfortable on a sofa in the front room, and he had drifted off to sleep.

The outlaw we had surprised behind the house, just before Hostler took care of him, was in the corner with his hands tied. Now he had a headache to go with his sore shoulder. I had told him we would take him in to see the doctor before he went to jail. He had nodded, then stared a long time at the bodies of Diehl and the other outlaw. We had loaded them onto horses to take them to town for burial.

"We need to know what we're facing when we get to town," I told the others on the porch. Pike Hardy looked over at the outlaw in the corner.

"What's your name?" he asked.

"Shorty," he answered finally.

I walked over to stand in front of Shorty. "Maybe, Shorty," I said, "you can tell us who is in town that we need to be thinkin' about."

Shorty took one more look at the corpses loaded on horses in the yard. He swallowed, leaned forward, and grimaced. "You'll get me to a doc like you promised, right?"

"We'll have the doc look at that shoulder just as soon as we get to town," I said.

"I know what the plan was three days ago," Shorty said. "There was a guy called himself Jenkins, Slade Jenkins. He was gonna get hisself made temporary sheriff in Fredericksburg 'cause you been gone."

Shorty stopped and looked at me. "You're McCabe, right?" he asked. I nodded and waited.

"Jenkins had another gunhand he called Charlie. He took Charlie to town with him. Plus, Diehl had a bruiser he called Boots. Jenkins took Boots." He stopped and took a drink of water when I offered it. "Boots got his name 'cause he likes to stomp on people. He don't wear a gun most of the time. Wants to beat people with his fists."

Shorty stopped and took another drink, then leaned back. "The two you just killed were named Diehl and Bryce. That's all I know," he said.

I'd been sheriff long enough to get a pretty good sense of when people were telling me the truth, and my gut told me Shorty had told us everything he knew. I looked around the circle and stood up.

"I'd like to take Hardy and Hostler with me," I said. "We should be able to take care of things in town." I turned around to look at them. "By the way," I said, "I have just deputized you boys."

Julie walked me out to my horse and gave me a kiss. "I won't ask what you plan to do," she said. "Just come back safe and sound."

———

The man Jenkins called Charlie was on a mission this morning. He was carrying a message from Jenkins to Diehl about what had happened in town, then he was to report back to Jenkins.

His real name was Woody, but he answered to Charlie as long as he got paid. If he stopped getting paid, or the deal got too risky, he would ride on, just like he always did. The way he saw things, if Jenkins could keep the sheriff job for a while, they could make some good money. If that didn't work out, he would fold his hand here and ride north somewhere.

Charlie was lost in his thoughts as he rode toward the stone house where Diehl would have taken over by now. When he heard voices coming from somewhere down the trail, he reined in and pulled off into the trees. He muzzled his horse to keep the animal quiet and waited.

He didn't have long to wait. Three men came around the corner. The big man in front wore a badge. Behind the three of them came two horses with dead men slung over and tied down. It wasn't hard to figure out the dead men were Diehl and Bryce.

Charlie stood and watched until the party rode around the bend and disappeared from view. He led his horse back out to the trail and stood there for quite a while. Finally, he mounted up and rode away. He would take the road north. He'd heard that a man could make money up in the Nation. It was time to find out if that was true.

———

We split up at the edge of town. I sent Hardy and Hostler to the sheriff's office. I had a feeling Jenkins had that thug Boots doing his dirty work, collecting money, while Jenkins did nothing. I told Hardy to get the drop on Jenkins and put him in his own jail.

Hardy nodded. "If Jenkins wants to get rough with us?" he asked.

I glanced over at him. "I'm guessin' you learned how to deal with sort of thing in the Army," I said.

Hardy chuckled. "I believe I did," he agreed.

I stayed for a minute after they rode away. I decided to ride down Main Street for a while, then check the saloons for Boots. I wanted folks to know I was back in town. A few people came over to welcome me back as I rode, and a few looked at me and hurried on. They wanted no trouble, I guess.

I stopped at two saloons without finding Boots, though the owner at the second saloon told me Boots had been in that morning to demand money.

I moved down to the general store, and there I saw a big man in a dirty vest walking out of the store, stuffing money into his pocket. Behind him, I saw the storekeeper sitting on the floor, bleeding from the mouth, looking dazed. I knew I had found Boots.

Boots saw me crossing the street and took in my badge and my Colt with one glance. Moving faster than I would have given him credit for, he leaped to one side, grabbed a lady passing by the store, pulled a knife from his belt and held it to her throat.

———

Jenkins sat behind the desk in the sheriff's office, counting the money from his first day on the job. Boots was really good at collecting money, he had to admit. And, when Charlie got back from the ranch, he expected to put a couple of his gunhands out on the road, relieving stagecoaches and other folks of their money.

The door opened, and Jenkins looked up to see two strangers. The one in front was taller and held a Winchester. Jenkins's eyes dropped to the man's belt. He had a Colt besides the rifle. The man in the back wore a pistol but didn't carry a rifle. Jenkins's eyes moved over to a peg on the wall, where he'd hung his gun belt when he came in.

Jenkins sat up and looked at the strangers. "What can I do for you boys?" he asked. One hand dropped below the desk. There was a gun in the side drawer. He held eye contact with the one in front while he slowly reached toward the drawer.

"We're sheriff's deputies, here to arrest you," the first one answered.

Jenkins stared. His hand stopped moving. "I'm the sheriff," he barked, "and you ain't my deputies."

"Not your deputies," the tall one agreed. "We're

deputies to Jake McCabe. The real sheriff. He's back in town."

Jenkins's hand shot out. He grabbed the desk drawer and yanked it open. He reached inside the drawer, searching for the gun. The man leaped forward and slammed the drawer shut on his fingers as he screamed in pain. When he felt a gun barrel against his temple, he held still and placed his other hand on top of the desk.

"Good choice," said Pike Hardy. He turned to the second man. "Hostler," he said, "let's see if one of the keys on that ring over there fits a jail cell."

———

I stopped where I was, watching Boots. He circled around a bit, getting the girl between him and my gun.

"What do you want?" I asked. "You know that if you hurt that girl, you'll die a couple seconds later."

Boots stared at me, eyes darting down to my gun and back. "There's another sheriff, now," he told me. "Mebbe I'll just wait for him to come and take care of you."

"Nope," I said flatly. "He's plumb out of business by now."

He watched me, trying to decide whether he believed me. His eyes darted down the street, then back. "Okay," he said, "here's what I want. You take off that gun and I let go of the girl and drop the knife. You an' me go at it. Knuckle and skull, right here. I win, you let me go. You win, you take me to jail."

I thought that one over, then reached for my gunbelt and unbuckled it. I held it out, but kept the pistol within reach. He lowered the knife, but kept hold of it. "Count of three," I said. "I drop the gunbelt and you drop the knife."

He nodded slowly, and I counted it down. When I reached three, we both dropped our weapons. The girl scrambled to safety, and we moved to the middle of the street. A crowd formed around us.

Boots laughed, raising his fists. "You're a fool," he said.

I said nothing. I just circled and watched. I'd fought guys like this before. If you got 'em mad, they would rush and try to take you out with one punch. "You gonna fight?" I asked, "or are you just gonna talk me to death?"

He bellowed and came at me, swinging a heavy right fist. I stepped to my right and jolted him hard with a left hand to his right eye. He wheeled around, swinging again with both hands, first right, then left. I stepped inside his punches and delivered a hard overhand right that smashed him in the mouth. He fell to one knee, fished around in his mouth and came out with a broken tooth.

I stepped back and waited, circling just a little. He reached down for a handful of dirt, but I had seen that one before. When he came off the ground, I stepped in and smashed him in the right eye again. He gasped, and the dirt dropped from his hand.

His right eye was swollen and starting to bleed. I was pretty sure he was having trouble seeing out of that one, so I kept circling to his right. He charged me, trying to get his hands around my throat. I stepped aside, grasped my hands together and brought them down like a club on the back of his head as he went by. He went to his knees.

He was finished, but this kind would only go down punching. I stood behind him and waited. He came off the ground with a roar and spun around, swinging that massive right hand again. I sidestepped his punch and swung a right uppercut that started down around my knees and finished on the point of his jaw.

His momentum kept him going, but he fell forward onto his face like a sack of feed hitting the ground. He didn't move.

A familiar voice came to me from the crowd. "That's the problem with you, McCabe. You never leave nuthin' for the rest of us to do."

I looked over and saw Leander McNelly grinning at me.

"Well," I said. "You can throw him in jail if you've a mind to. I'm a little tuckered out now."

CHAPTER 20

PASSING THE TORCH

THREE WEEKS LATER

My father-in-law Ike knows how to throw a shindig when he wants to, no doubt about that. He waited a little while, until things had settled and Boone was feeling better, but then he roasted a whole ox and invited half the town out to the ranch.

I'd had Pike Hardy helping me in the sheriff's office the whole time, seeing as how Boone wasn't up to it yet, and Ike had plenty to do at the ranch. Pike hadn't pushed me about things, but I could tell he wanted it settled. He wanted to know if it was permanent.

I waited until things had settled down a bit, then went and pulled up a chair next to Boone. That old codger always knew what I was thinkin'. It was a little scary sometimes.

"First of all," he said, "I'm upset you went to town and fought Boots without me havin' a chance to get some bets down."

I rolled my eyes and waited.

"You gonna make Pike your new deputy?" he asked.

"That depends on you," I told him. "The job is yours as long as you want it. We been through a lot together."

Boone grinned and looked over at Alice. "She wants to me to settle down and herd cows 'cause it's dangerous work sheriffin'." He stopped and took a pull at the beer he was holding. "I think it's time," he said. "I didn't move on when I thought you still needed me, but Pike Hardy has some bark on him. He'll watch out for you. Let him be your deputy now."

We shook hands on it and I moved over to where Pike Hardy sat, pounding down a big plate of beef. He'd been watching me talk to Boone, and I thought he might know what was coming, too.

I pulled a deputy's badge out of my pocket. "It's yours to wear if you want to," I told him. "Permanent. I'd be pleased to have you join me."

Hardy grinned, picked up the badge, and fastened it to his vest pocket. He studied it for a minute. "I think it suits me," he said.

Julia walked over, carrying just about the biggest piece of apple pie I had ever seen, and put it down in front of Pike. "Congratulations, deputy," she told him. "The next thing is I'm going to help find you a girl."

Hardy looked up at Julia, then at me. His mouth worked open and shut a couple of times, but he didn't manage to say anything. "You might just as well let her help," I said. "She's hard to stop once she gets started."

Julia stepped back and took my hand. "You never know, you might be the sheriff before long, Pike," she told him.

Just before she stepped away, she leaned over and

whispered in my ear. "Because," she said, "new daddies need to stay around home a little more and not get themselves punched and shot at."

I stared at her. She just chuckled and walked away.

———————

Pike Hardy was still there in the yard at the ranch long after the others had left. For now, he was living in the bunkhouse at the Hawkins/McCabe ranch, and that suited him just fine. He walked into the bunkhouse, took off his badge, and set it on a table next to his bunk. He went back outside and stood there for a long time, just enjoying the evening.

Funny, he thought, how things turned out. Just a year ago, he hadn't even thought about leaving the Army. Now, he had mustered out, moved to Texas, and taken a job as a deputy sheriff. Maybe, he thought, this was the start of a lot of things. A lot of good things, in a new life, with a new future.

A Look At:

Fredericksburg Law: The Story of Pike Hardy

What does a veteran of the frontier army do once he musters out?

For Pike Hardy, the answer is a fresh start in the booming frontier town of Fredericksburg, Texas. With his old friend Jake McCabe retiring as sheriff, Pike hopes for a smooth transition into his new role. But life on the Texas frontier is never that easy.

From battling moonshiners and facing an old enemy to dealing with a sharp-tongued girl from back East who wants nothing to do with him, Pike must learn fast if he wants to survive—and keep the peace. Luckily for Fredericksburg, Pike Hardy is a quick study.

This two-volume bundle includes both Pike Hardy *and* Shadow of Sam Bass.

AVAILABLE SEPTEMBER 2025

ABOUT THE AUTHOR

Patrick Lindsay came to Texas by way of Missouri, Canada, and California and has been proud to call the Lone Star State his home for more than forty years now. He retired in 2017 from "another life" as a CPA, whereafter he turned his hand to writing.

He has read just about everything by Louis L'Amour and first decided to give Western writing a try on his initial day of retirement. He has been writing ever since and loves the idea that so many people get enjoyment from his work.

Patrick and his wife Michelle live on a cattle ranch near Fort Worth along with cows, horses, chickens, and a very spoiled Great Pyrenees dog. He is an avid fan of the St. Louis Cardinals in baseball and the Kansas City Chiefs in football.